CUT TO THE BONE

CHAINS OF COMMAND BOOK 3

ZEN DIPIETRO

COPYRIGHT

COPYRIGHT © 2018 BY ZEN DIPIETRO

This is a work of fiction. Names, characters, organizations, events, and incidents are either products of the author's imagination or used fictitiously. Any resemblance to actual events, business establishments, locales, or persons, living or dead, is coincidental.

All rights reserved. No part of this publication may be reproduced, stored in a retrieval system, or transmitted in any form or by any means (electronic, mechanical, photocopying, recording, or otherwise) without express written permission of the publisher. The only exception is brief quotations for the purpose of review.

Please purchase only authorized electronic editions. Distribution of this book via the Internet or via any other means without the permission of the publisher is illegal and punishable by law.

ISBN: 978-1-943931-33-0 (paperback)

Published in the United States of America by Parallel Worlds Press

Cover art by Zen DiPietro

DRAGONFIRE STATION UNIVERSE

Original Series (complete)
Dragonfire Station Book 1: Translucid
Dragonfire Station Book 2: Fragments
Dragonfire Station Book 3: Coalescence

Intersections (Dragonfire Station Short Stories)

Mercenary Warfare series (complete)
Selling Out
Blood Money
Hell to Pay
Calculated Risk
Going for Broke

Chains of Command series
New Blood
Blood and Bone
Cut to the Bone
Out for Blood

To get updates on releases and sales, sign up for Zen's newsletter at www.ZenDiPietro.com.

1

Fallon felt like her legs had been torn off.

Being separated from her team wasn't exactly a physical pain. It was more of a feeling of being incomplete and less capable than she was accustomed to. A deep, constant ache chewed at her every hour she was awake.

Why had PAC command made her, Peregrine, Hawk, and Raptor into such a tight-knit team only to pull them apart like this?

She hated it.

It would have been easy to let herself sink into that feeling, or even become depressed. Doing that wouldn't serve her teammates, though, or the PAC, so she vowed to force herself to focus only on the job ahead of her.

It wasn't an easy task, trying to convince herself not to feel bereft.

During the first month of traveling across the galaxy with Minho to her new post, she felt like she was one big, open wound despite her best efforts.

She wasn't accustomed to her best efforts failing.

The second month, her sensation of rawness transitioned into a welcome, dull numbness.

Finally, in the third month, as the ship traveled further away from Earth than she'd ever been, she was finally able to put all of her energies into preparing for her job on Asimov Station, which had recently reached the final stages of its construction. It would become the newest, most state-of-the-art installation in the PAC.

She would accomplish the mission then return to her team as efficiently as possible. That was how she could best serve Avian Unit and the Planetary Alliance Cooperative. She aimed all her effort and attention at this goal. Now that she'd completed officer training school, her unique version of security training would be the setup of Asimov's security system, from installation to final checks. If she had been a typical security officer, she'd have had a much more structured internship that worked through an established curriculum. Instead, she would dive elbow-deep into intensive hardware installation, software checks, creating evacuation plans and emergency protocols, and, eventually, running security drills.

Trial by fire.

She'd be going all-in for her very first foray into the specialty. Since it was an exciting project, she felt eager to tackle it, rather than intimidated by it.

Gazing out the porthole at Asimov Station, she imagined working there alongside Minho. A great deal of critical labor lay ahead of them, hovering in a somewhat out-of-the-way portion of PAC space.

Minho would, as he always did, make it all manageable. He'd been a great help to her during the past three months. He had a certain astuteness that he artfully blended with deft subtlety. He'd frequently used those skills to take her mind off her isolation from her team. No doubt he'd do the same when they tackled the monumental task directly ahead of them.

The voyage had given them time to immerse themselves in intensive study of cutting-edge security systems. Then, they debated the best plan for Asimov. As they approached the station itself, they had a fully-developed, clear plan of action.

They were ready to get to work.

She was grateful for Minho's quiet support, and glad for the chance to get to know him better. They brought out the competitive and often playful parts of each other, and their personalities meshed extremely well. She couldn't have picked a better-suited travel companion for herself even if she'd been given the opportunity to try.

She had gotten the opportunity to see Bennaris, which had been their last stop before arriving at Asimov. Fallon found the planet to be just as lovely as Val, her friend from the academy, had described. The funny thing about looking at images of other places on the voicecom was that it never accurately portrayed the feel of a place. Certain nuances just had to be experienced in real time.

One planet visited, hundreds of others in the Planetary Alliance Cooperative still to see.

"What are you doing?" Minho's voice made her turn away from the porthole.

"Looking at Asimov Station," she said. "Putting the mental image of it into our plans so I can adjust what I'd envisioned. Voicecom images never quite convey the same feeling of actually being somewhere."

He moved past her to get a packet of lemonade out of the cooler. "But why are you doing it in the galley? The view from your room would be the same."

She shrugged. "It was a chance to stretch my legs. I'm more than ready for new surroundings."

He took a sip of his drink. "I don't love long space flights either, but you'll get used to them. They're part of the job."

She turned and leaned against the bulkhead. "I'm not used to having so much time on my hands. I'd have taken more time at the helm if the pilots had let me."

"Just because you didn't have a rigid schedule doesn't mean you didn't have a lot to accomplish. But I can see how, after the academy and officer training school, not having a regimented schedule would feel strange. After this trip and mission, you'll be expected to take daily shifts sitting at navigation. You got a pass this time around since you're new to long flights and because you had a lot to learn about the job on Asimov Station."

The PAC pilots who had been assigned to the flight, Henry and Jill, had been friendly but very restrained. Apparently, they'd been given strict orders to avoid crossing paths with Minho and Fallon whenever possible.

It had kept the pilots at a distance from them, making Minho her only source of companionship.

It was a good thing they got along so well.

"I learned a lot," she said. "I even had some time to pick up another language."

"Which one?"

"Rescan. I thought it might come in handy for security purposes, just in case some traders are speaking it because they assume I won't understand."

He raised his eyebrows, looking amused and maybe just a smidge impressed. "That's a good idea. How many languages do you know?"

"That makes seven. I'll keep adding, though. How many do you speak?"

He switched to speaking in Rescan. "Four, fluently, including Standard. Learning the other three took tremendous effort. I can get by in two or three others, but I can't speak anything like a native. Languages aren't really my thing."

That shouldn't surprise her, but it did. Many people only

spoke Standard, since all PAC planets used it, often in place of their own native language. But she and Minho were so similar, it surprised her to find a significant difference between them.

"Don't look so disappointed," he laughed.

"I'm not," she denied quickly. "Your Rescan is really good. You almost speak like a native."

"Oh, only 'almost.'" He pantomimed a knife to his heart, pretending to be in terrible pain.

She laughed.

"Look." He gestured to the porthole.

They were about to dock.

Finally. She was ready to get to work. The sooner she got this job done, the sooner she could rejoin her team.

She wondered where Hawk, Peregrine, and Raptor were, and what their new assignments were. They could be as close as Bennaris, as far as she knew, or at the very edge of the PAC zone, in the Barony Coalition or something.

She had no way of knowing where they were. Her orders had been clear that she was not to attempt to contact any of them during this assignment, nor speak to them afterward about it.

She willed her partners to complete their missions well, and as soon as possible.

In the meantime, she'd give this assignment her all, so she could learn whatever PAC command, Blackout, and especially Admiral Krazinski wanted her to learn. The project would be intensive, but she and Minho had broken it down into sequential tasks on a schedule that would allow them to have the job done on time.

She only hoped the work would be as straightforward as it seemed.

An EAGER-TO-PLEASE young lieutenant greeted them at the airlock. She enthusiastically escorted them through the station.

Fallon wasn't an expert on space stations, having only visited two, but Asimov felt—and smelled—very different than Jamestown or Dragonfire. As she stepped onto the new station, she tried to identify what made it so different.

Both of the established stations had felt as alive as any city she'd visited. People bustled from one place to another and others lingered about, socializing with one another. Conversation and laughter rang out. There had been a feeling of life going on in a thousand different ways, creating a nexus of time and space in a way that humanized a giant hunk of technology hanging in the void of space. Dragonfire and Jamestown had felt like communities, just like a town on a planet.

Asimov Station didn't have any of that going for it just yet. It felt like a hunk of technology.

The idea of helping to make Asimov ready to become a community made her feel good. Useful.

The lieutenant gestured at the corridor. Much of it had exposed hardware lining the bulkheads. "As you can see, Asimov Station has been engineered with all the latest technology. Conductive materials in places where it can help conserve energy, and nonconductive materials in areas where heat needs to be controlled. High efficiency materials in every single system and component."

Lieutenant Lee seemed enthusiastic. She somehow seemed younger than Fallon, even though Lee's record proved her to be five years older.

"Have you been aboard a space station before, Lieutenant Arashi?" Lee asked.

Arashi would be her name here, as it had been at OTS. Lieutenant Emiko Arashi, security specialist. Fallon had fixed Minho's fictional identity for this mission into her brain, as well. Here, he would be Lieutenant Commander Minho Park, also a security specialist and her direct superior.

Fallon's faux biography included a couple of short stints on stations, so she felt confident about answering, "Yes, I have, though not long-term. I understand you've been here for a while now."

Lieutenant Lee nodded. "Yes, I've been here since slightly before Asimov was habitable. It's a long-term assignment for me. Once the command crew arrives, I'll become its most junior member."

The lieutenant made a visible effort to mute her pride but didn't entirely succeed. She glowed with enthusiasm.

"Your first command position?" Minho asked.

"Yup. Eventually, I want to captain one of these. This is my first big step."

Minho smiled. "No wonder you requested such a lonely assignment. Not a lot of people would want to be on a station for months with only a skeleton crew."

"Sometimes I wish for a little bit of night life," Lee admitted, "but it's been an interesting experience. And the crew will arrive before long. We're getting close."

Fallon reached out and slid her fingertip across a section of finished bulkhead. "It's interesting to see a station in such pristine condition. I'm sure this assignment will be a learning experience for me, too."

Lee smiled, and Fallon expected to like this ambitious, hard-working officer who showed all of her feelings in her expressions and body language. She seemed like a very honest, forthright person.

Working with someone like that might be a refreshing change of pace.

Lieutenant Lee nodded. "I'm sure it will be. I still learn something new every day. I'll show you to your quarters first. You can rest if you're tired. I'm not sure what day cycle you're used to, but we're following the PAC standard schedule here already. You can take some time to adjust if you need to."

"No need," Minho answered. "We're already on a standard cycle, and since it's only midday, we can just drop off our belongings and get right to the tour of the station. I don't know about Lieutenant Arashi here, but after months in space, I'm glad to have a change of scenery."

Fallon nodded in emphatic agreement.

"Great," Lieutenant Lee said, sounding pleased. "The good news is that since we don't have many people here, that makes us the ranking officers, and we can stay in the best accommodations." She laughed.

"That sounds fun," Fallon admitted. "I'd enjoy some room to spread out. I've been in tight confines for quite a while now."

She didn't just mean the ship. Before that, she'd shared living quarters with her team, and before that, she'd had a tiny dorm room.

Having a lot of space to herself suddenly sounded like a grand luxury.

When they arrived at the quarters, she wasn't disappointed. Her room was right next to Minho's and they looked mostly the same. An ergonomic design made the most of an already-generous space. Fallon set her bags on the dining table that slid out from the wall and admired the sleek, minimalistic décor.

Whoever got stationed here long-term would no doubt personalize the space in their own way, but for Fallon's taste, this was an ideal set-up. The furniture looked comfortable, and nothing drew any particular attention.

She appreciated simplicity.

"What a restful space," she said. "I like it."

"Really?" Lieutenant Lee asked before catching herself and ducking her head in embarrassment. "I mean, it's nice. I'd want to add some bright colors, though."

"I'm sure that would be good too," Fallon said, "but simple suits me."

"Me too," Minho said. "I'm sure we'll be very comfortable here. Since we've both dropped off our things, what should we see next?"

Lee brightened. "Everything."

2

LIEUTENANT LEE HADN'T BEEN KIDDING when she said she wanted to show them 'everything.' With great enthusiasm, she showed Fallon and Minho every section of the station, from the lifts to the air containment system to ops control.

Though they'd met a few crew and service workers along the way, the three of them stood alone in the large control center of the station.

And there was the command chair. Unoccupied. A sensation Fallon had never experienced swept over her.

She couldn't help but look at the chair.

"Go ahead." Minho nudged her.

She nudged him back. "You're the senior officer here. If someone's going to sit, it should be you."

He smiled. Minho had a great smile. The expression didn't just come from his lips, but from his eyes and the rounding of his cheeks. All his good humor came out when he smiled. "I've sat in the command chair before. It's fine, but I don't really get a thrill out of it."

He nudged her again. "Do it. You know you want to."

She glanced at Lieutenant Lee, who grinned and said, "Give it a try. I did it, too, when I first got here."

Well, if her subordinate had done it, then why not?

Fallon turned, let out a breath, and sat.

She imagined herself as captain of the station, snapping out orders and being obeyed without question. She envisioned the station as a hive of activity—efficient and productive.

Yeah, that was a good feeling.

"Ohh, you're one of the ones who likes it. I had a feeling you would be." Minho grinned. "Some people are made for a command chair."

She sent him a look of amused disdain. "Don't make me send you to the brig."

He grinned and shifted his weight. It was subtle, but she recognized it as the balance of someone who was ready to fight. A private, unspoken joke between the two of them.

Still grinning, he said, "You can try."

She laughed.

Lieutenant Lee watched them with curiosity and amusement. "You two must know each other pretty well already."

"We've worked together," Minho said in a tone that sounded like an agreement, but without providing any specifics. "We also had the whole trip here, so poor Arashi here has had to suffer a lot of my company."

Fallon admired his lowkey artfulness at appearing to be open while actually revealing nothing. She made a mental note for her future use. In fact, she'd contribute right then by changing the subject.

She stood. "It's a fine station. Thank you for showing us around. How do you organize mealtimes here?"

Lieutenant Lee retrieved her comport from her belt and checked the chronometer. "Good timing. Since there are so few of us here now, we've set a specific hour for breakfast, lunch, and dinner. We show up if we aren't too busy, and it gives us a chance to talk to others in person rather than just on the voicecom. It'll be nice to have some new voices adding to the conversation."

She gestured for them to follow her. "Remember that place I pointed out on the boardwalk? We've set it up as a temporary galley until some restaurant owner moves in. It's mostly just food in packets that we put into the heat-ex, but there are some basic cooking ingredients, too. We also have a fledgling hydroponics bay that's just starting to offer some mushrooms, peppers, and tomatoes on a very limited basis."

She paused to give them a hopeful look. "Do either of you cook?"

Fallon shook her head, but Minho nodded. "Yeah, I like it."

Lee looked delighted. "Oh, fantastic! Maybe you can treat us to a meal or two. Packets get boring after a while."

Minho nodded good-naturedly. "Maybe. We'll have to see what the pantry looks like."

Forty minutes later, Fallon, Lee, and Minho—along with a half dozen other people—dug into a stir-fried vegetable and noodle dish.

"This is way better than the pre-made noodles," Lee said. "What did you do?"

Minho shrugged off the praise. "I just sautéed some mushrooms and zucchini, and added black bean paste and seasonings. It's nothing, really."

"They should change the noodle packet to taste like this," said a mechanical engineer they'd just met. He was the youngest of the group and seemed to take the frequent teasing of his colleagues with good humor.

"Thanks, Ensign Arrem." Minho took another bite. "But then how would I impress my co-workers with relatively little effort or skill?"

They all chuckled as they continued to eat. Fallon admired

Minho's easy way of talking to people. She was sure he was already well-liked. She had always had a much harder time meeting and getting to know people.

Lieutenant Lee pushed her empty tray aside. "We're all on a first-name basis here, since it doesn't make sense to stand on formality with so few of us here. Of course, we'll use your titles if you prefer it, but feel free to call us all by our first names."

Minho swiped at the corner of his mouth with his thumb. "Fine by me. I'm not much for formality, myself. Of course, Lieutenant Arashi here is a terrible stickler, and a general killjoy, so she'll probably ruin it for everyone."

All eyes turned to Fallon. She stared at Minho in surprise, but quickly realized that he wanted her to make more of an effort with making conversation.

She laughed lightly. "He's joking. He does that. He thinks he's funny." She made a humorous face, squinting one eye. "Mostly, we just keep letting him think it."

Chuckles went around the room and she could see everyone relaxing.

"Feel free to call me Emiko, of course," she added.

Lieutenant Lee—no, her first name was Katheryn—quickly said, "When we have visitors, we revert to standard protocol. It's just simpler to keep it casual while we're getting the station ready."

"How often do you get visitors?" Fallon asked.

Jacen Arrem said, "Depends. Sometimes it's weeks between, and sometimes we have back-to-back inspections. We even had a ship that needed an emergency docking for repairs."

"They were lucky you were equipped enough for that," Minho noted.

Jacen nodded. "Yeah. There's a reason this station was built here. It's a long way to the next outpost. If not for Asimov Station, they'd have had to try to make it to Bennaris."

"I don't think they would have," a mechanical contractor named Jess Barkin said. She wasn't an officer, but she must have had a lot of experience because her job was to oversee much of the physical work being done. At forty-six, she was the oldest person on the skeleton crew. "They'd have started experiencing cascade failures within forty-eight hours if we hadn't been here."

"I bet they were mighty grateful," Minho said.

Jacen shrugged. "They were Rescan traders, so mostly they were concerned about making it to their trade on time, and how much we'd charge them for our assistance."

Minho wiped his mouth with a napkin, then dropped it on his empty tray and sat back. "You never know with visitors. They could be great, they could be awful. Best case scenario in either case is that they're up front and you figure out what you're dealing with. Hopefully you all have decided that Emiko and I will be fairly tolerable to have around."

Chuckles and nods indicated that the consensus approved of the newcomers.

Jess gathered her cup, tray, and chopsticks and stood. "Thanks for the dinner. I should get back to work. The sooner we get this bucket put together, the sooner I can get home." She paused. "No offense to those of you who plan to stay long-term."

Katheryn Lee, along with a tech in his twenties who had remained fairly silent throughout the meal, both waved her off.

Fallon was glad to see that the crew didn't seem inclined toward formality or high-maintenance social etiquette. It would be a lot tougher to work here if people were quick to take offense.

But then, they had probably been chosen for this assignment because they were well-suited to it, both in terms of skill and temperament.

Fallon stood and hid her amusement when Katheryn started to rise and bow to her as a senior officer, then realized what she was doing and pretended she was adjusting the strap on her shoe.

That Katheryn was a go-getter, for sure, and might very well climb the chain of command quickly.

Minho reached for Fallon's tray and cup, stacked them with his, and efficiently washed them up. She suspected he was making a point of not expecting any special treatment as the senior officer. When he was done, he said, "I think I'll retire for the night. Then Emiko and I will work the day shift tomorrow. Let us know if you need anything or just want to hang out."

Fallon nodded. "I'm ready to turn in, too. It was great to meet you all. Our paths might not cross a lot, since we'll be working on the security system, but I'll definitely meet up for meals whenever I can. Or if anyone plays games in the evening, I like cards and *Go*. Or I'm always open to learning something new."

She got all-around smiles for that offer, so she knew she'd made a good choice.

"Sleep well," Katheryn called.

"Don't let the spacebugs bite," Jacen said, grinning. Apparently, he liked to make fun of the fact that he was the youngest.

Emiko smiled at him, and she thought she detected a hint of pink on his cheeks.

Uh oh. She'd have to be careful to discourage a crush, if he turned out to be inclined toward one. She didn't need that kind of complication in her life. She had plenty to keep her busy as it was.

"OH, THIS IS SWEET." Fallon couldn't help but feel excited about the groundwork that had been laid for the security features of Asimov Station. Seeing how neatly the new systems had been designed was a treat.

Maybe, if she hadn't decided to be a Blackout officer, she might have made a good security officer, after all.

Minho grinned at her. "You like that?"

"Bleeding edge technology that I can use to protect this station, as well as study for the purpose of infiltrating in the future? Oh yeah. I like it." She eyed the voicecom panel with greedy eagerness.

Minho laughed. "I guess the higher-ups know what they're doing when they pick people for particular things."

She made a slashing gesture at him. "Pontificate later. Right now, let's dig into this."

Two hours later, she'd memorized the classified plans, and she and Minho had gotten right to work.

"Ever been inside a service conduit?" Minho asked as they grabbed components and toolkits and headed to their first location.

"Nope," Fallon said.

"Well, you're a pilot, so you can't be claustrophobic, but just remember not to move too quickly or else you'll bang your elbows, knees, or head. Maybe even all of the above."

She laughed. "Seriously?"

"You'd be surprised."

AFTER THREE HOURS inside the cramped confines of service conduits, Fallon understood what Minho had meant about the restrictive confines.

"Blood and bone," she muttered to herself wryly as she adjusted her hips and shoulders into an odd posture so she could force open an access panel.

It wasn't just the tight space, though, that made her consider every movement. She didn't mind that. The sound was what bothered her. Something about being in such a small, confined area made sounds louder and more abrupt. Even the sound of her sliding along on her back and elbows sounded oddly loud.

But somehow, when Minho spoke from only yards away, he sounded like he was on the other end of a tunnel.

As a result, she found she preferred not to talk while working.

She developed a routine for installing the security sensors. Install, connect, activate, test. Over and over.

When they finished with that particular area of the station and exited the conduit, she slid into the corridor with a sense of relief. Her knees definitely felt the effects of crawling through the tunnels, and so did her shoulders.

"Ready to quit?" Minho shifted his toolkit to his other hand to elbow her playfully.

She smiled. "Hardly. If I can take a Hawk punch to the chest, I can deal with some conduit work."

He hitched his head toward the south. "Let's put the tools away, then I'll treat you to dinner."

"Treat, huh?" She fell into step beside him. "Going to order delivery?"

They laughed.

"Sure," he said. "How about some Bennite stew, fresh from Bennaris? Everything has a price. I bet it could be done."

She laughed, imagining how much the bill would be to have food delivered a three-day flight away. "How about you show me some of your packet doctoring tricks, instead?"

"Wow, you're a cheap date. I like that." He winked at her.

She rolled her eyes, grinning.

"I squirreled away some good stuff in my quarters this morning. The kitchenette is pretty nice for cooking, too. I had a feeling we'd miss the regular dinner hour, so we're all set."

"I like that you planned ahead." She followed him to return their tools, then they continued on to his quarters. Upon arriving, they went straight to the kitchenette to wash their hands and get to work.

"When did you take up cooking?" she asked.

He spoke without looking at her, his eyes on an onion he was reducing to tiny, precisely-sized pieces with a sharp knife. "I did a little of it as a kid, but I started doing more during the academy. I get bored quickly with the lack of variety from packet meals, plus it's nice to do something so basic. It can be relaxing after a day of doing complicated things."

"Plus, you get the chance to eat without running into anyone and having to make small talk," she added. "I like the people here so far, but sometimes I just don't want to talk."

"Yep," he said. "You're very disagreeable. You'll need to work on that."

She laughed. "I am not. I just like my space. Not everyone is as sociable as you."

He put the onions into the heat-ex and activated the grill setting. "I'm kidding. You do fine when you choose to. That's all that matters—that you can turn it on and use it when you need to."

She'd expected more teasing, not an actual compliment.

Well, it was sort of a compliment. She chose to see it as such, anyway.

"Thanks. What should I do with this?" She held up the small packets of spice he'd used to season some vegetables.

He pointed to a drawer, then opened the cooler and surveyed the contents with a dissatisfied expression. "I wish they'd stocked the station with more basic ingredients. I'd rather cook dried pasta than use packets."

With a shrug and a sigh, he pulled out two noodle packets. He took the onions out of the heat-ex, changed the setting, and inserted the packets.

"Probably by the time the crew arrives, they'll have a wider variety of items," she said, putting the spices away.

"Yeah," he agreed. "But that's two months away. And we're going to have to work our asses off to get the security in place before they arrive, so we can immediately start running security drills."

"Why such a tight schedule?" she asked. "They could have had someone else put in the security, instead of having to wait until we arrived."

"That's why all the basics are already in place," he said. "Not only does it protect the station from anyone who might try to seize control of it, it laid the groundwork for us."

Something about the way he said that caught her attention. "Us? Why us, though?"

He turned around and leaned back against the counter so he could look at her directly. "That's the other part of this assignment. Yes, you'll get expertise in security systems and their maintenance, and station protocols, but there's something bigger we need to do."

When he paused, she prompted, "What?"

"The captain," he said. "Phillip Lydecker. Once he arrives, he'll be our commanding officer. At least, he'll be the commanding officer of the people we're pretending to be. But even as we defer to him and give him our bows, we'll be investigating him for suspected smuggling."

She blinked at him in surprise. "Well, that certainly sounds more exciting than crawling through conduits for the next couple of months. Why is he under suspicion?"

"Too many coincidences," Minho said. "Goods that have been in places where he was stationed ended up somewhere they shouldn't have been. People who have crossed his path have also crossed the paths of unsavory types."

"So there's nothing concrete," she concluded. "Just innuendo and coincidence."

He nodded and removed the noodles from the heat-ex. "The PAC has no tolerance for officers who abuse their positions. Our job is either to exonerate him or prove his guilt."

The technical parts of this assignment had interested her in an academic sense. But this...this was the real deal—a Blackout assignment.

A ball of excitement inflated in her chest.

"You got quiet all of a sudden." Minho turned to glance at her as he stirred the onions and vegetables into the noodles. He paused when he got a good look at her. "Why are you smiling like that?"

"Like what?" Was she smiling?

"Like a mouse who just wriggled into the cheese factory. But, like, a really crazy mouse who's been taking steroids or something. Don't smile like that, ever again," he said. "It's scary."

She laughed.

"Now, come over here. These noodles aren't going to stir themselves." He extended a pair of chopsticks to her.

She tried not to smile as she sat across from him at the table. She leaned down and scooped noodles into her mouth. "Mm. These are really good."

"You're smiling again." He narrowed his eyes at her in mock admonishment, even as he wore an amused expression. "You can't be that excited about noodles. Are you that thrilled about the PAC possibly having a smuggler as a captain?"

She relaxed and let her smile fully unfurl. "No, of course not. But the possibility of taking a traitor down…well, that's exactly what I signed up for."

He eyed her, and his lips turned up in a small smile. "Yeah. Me too. But we have a lot to do before we get to that point."

After putting a bite of vegetables into her mouth, she glanced at him. He was focused on his food, but something about him in that moment caught her attention.

She tried to identify it.

"What?" he asked.

"Nothing."

"You're looking at me," he said.

"You're the only other person here," she pointed out. "And therefore, the only person I could be looking at."

He arched an eyebrow at her, smiled, and continued eating.

Then it hit her. She realized what had made her keep looking at him. Familiarity. There was something about Minho that made him more like her than anyone she'd ever met.

She didn't know what to make of that, so she focused all of her attention on her noodles.

3

A week after her arrival on Asimov Station, Fallon had settled into a busy but comfortable routine. She and Minho worked the day shift, meeting for breakfast, getting right to work, and meeting up with the rest of the crew for lunch and dinner whenever their work for the day didn't make it too inconvenient.

She'd met up with a few of the crew to play cards twice, and suspected she'd proven herself well enough to continue getting invitations.

Evenings varied. She usually exercised after work, and Minho joined her every other day or so. If they didn't work out together, they might meet up to watch a holo-vid or something.

On that particular evening, she was on her own. No card-playing, no holo-vids with Minho, just her and the pleasant fatigue from a long day of installing security systems then a hard workout.

It was nice to have some time alone.

Since she'd missed dinner hour, she tried a little bit of Minho-inspired packet doctoring with some chicken salad and wide, salty crackers. It didn't turn out amazing, but it was edible.

Her fresh salad, though, turned out terrific, and she counted her efforts as a win.

Alone with her thoughts, she reflected on the progress of her work on Asimov as she ate. Afterward, she checked her messages on the voicecom, then sat in front of the holo-projector, only to decide she wasn't in the mood for a vid.

Of their own volition, her thoughts turned to her team.

Where had Peregrine been sent? Her specialties were disguises and small spyware devices. What kind of job would PAC command have her do?

Or Hawk? His specialties were shady connections, operating among those shady types, and brute force.

He could have gone pretty much anywhere. She hoped he was safe.

Then she thought of Raptor. He came to mind last because he was the one she tried the hardest not to think about. She missed him more than she wanted to. She missed his smile, his laugh, his sense of humor, and the way he cared about people.

Especially the way he cared about her.

Annoyed, Fallon stood and blew out a breath. These thoughts were dangerous. They could drag her down into melancholy. They could distract her from her work.

As much as she wanted to be with her team, dwelling on being apart from them would do no good. It would only hinder her from doing her best.

She wouldn't dishonor them by letting them become her weak spot. She needed to compartmentalize her feeling of loss. Lock it up and leave it in the dark.

"Right," she said to herself. "Maybe too much time to myself isn't such a great thing."

She checked the chronometer. She had two or three hours before she needed to sleep. She could go down to the engineering section and do some organizing to facilitate the next day's work.

Might as well be productive.

She quickly changed into a utility jumpsuit, pulled her hair back into a tight ponytail, and set out for engineering.

As she entered the main engineering room, someone stood up suddenly, looking startled. "Oh! Emiko. Hi."

Fallon immediately recognized him as twenty-year old Priestley Simkopf, the only member of the skeleton crew besides Lieutenant Katheryn Lee who intended to remain on the station once it was in operation.

"Sorry, did I surprise you?" she asked with an easy smile.

"A little," he admitted. "Not many people work this time of night."

"Then why are you here?" she asked, keeping her tone light to avoid making it sound accusatory.

Priestley shrugged. "I get insomnia sometimes. I figure I might as well be doing something useful, rather than tossing and turning in my bed."

She nodded understandingly. "I can relate to that, since I'm here for a similar reason. I figured, with nothing better to do with my time, I might as well get a jump start on tomorrow's work."

He smiled. "Yeah. I bet it's even more of a push for you to get it done, since you'll probably move on to something more long-term afterward."

He deactivated the voicecom panel in front of him and it went dark.

She searched her memory for his duty record and his purpose for being on this crew. She recalled that he had been brought on for all of the most menial tasks—cleanup, basic diagnostics, triple-checks of all systems, and so on. The super boring stuff no one wanted to do.

"Doing diagnostics?" she guessed.

He nodded. "Yeah. I have to make sure each panel is properly in sync with the core system."

"Are they ever not?" she asked.

"No," he said. "Not at this point. I'm largely superfluous. I'm just here for..." he searched for the right word, "redundancy."

She laughed. "I bet that's boring as hell."

He blinked in surprise, then laughed. "Uh, yeah, actually. At least if something needed fixing, I'd feel useful."

"It's a crap job nobody wants to do, but I'm guessing you took it so you could get a permanent position on Asimov. Is that right?"

He ducked his head self-consciously. "You got it. My background wasn't good enough to get hired on in the traditional way. They offered me a deal, though, so I figured it was worth it in the long term. I didn't go to university or anything, so it's a good opportunity for someone like me."

She didn't ask why he hadn't gotten schooling or training in some sort of trade. There were tons of possible reasons, and none of them were her business. "Well, it's nice to run into you. I haven't seen you around much for mealtimes."

He looked down again. He clearly lacked confidence. "Everyone's been pretty nice, but I feel like I don't belong. They're all specialists at something or other, even the ones who aren't officers. I'm just..." he shrugged. "The janitor, I guess."

"You're a bit more than that," she gently corrected. "Maintenance is a critical function, particularly on a self-contained structure like a space station. Anyone who would disrespect you for that doesn't deserve their own position. Let me know if that happens." She pressed her lips into a thin line. She had no tolerance for elitism.

His cheeks pinkened slightly. "It's nothing like that. But thank you. That's very kind of you."

"Not at all," she denied. "It's just fair, and what I expect of any duty station I work at."

He smiled faintly, then stood. "I'm done with my checks, so I'll leave you to get your work done. It was nice running into you."

"You too," she said. "I hope I'll see you again for mealtime soon."

He nodded and grabbed his toolkit before hurrying off.

She retrieved her own toolkit where she'd left it earlier that day. That set of tools was quite different from the set Priestley had carried.

She didn't mind his awkwardness. She understood it, sensing that he was an introvert, as she was. In general, she didn't crave interaction with other people, either.

Only certain people.

With determination, she set off for the conduit she and Minho would be working on next. She could probably get five or six sensors installed that evening, which would get them that much closer to completing this project.

Fallon had meant to work for two or three hours. However, once she got started with something, she had a tendency to become absorbed in it. As a result, she didn't close up the final conduit and pack up her tool kit until midnight.

She thought of the long trek to engineering to return the tools, then the walk back to her quarters. It would be easier if she could just take the kit to her room for the night and take it with her at the beginning of the next shift—which would begin in just a few hours.

But that would be breaking PAC regulations, and she had an example to set as a senior officer. Never mind that they were still setting up the station and it wasn't in regular use yet. PAC regulations were clear.

With a sigh, she set off for central engineering.

She strode down the corridor with a little less than her regular energy, and was surprised when Jess barreled around a corner and nearly bumped into her.

For an older woman, Jess moved fast.

"Oh, sorry!" Jess said, putting a hand on Fallon's shoulder to make sure she hadn't been unbalanced. She almost immediately realized that she now had her hand on an officer, and quickly snatched the hand back.

Fallon chuckled. "It's fine," she said easily, to make sure Jess knew she wasn't offended by the touch. "I didn't expect to see anyone, and I bet you didn't, either."

"Nope," Jess agreed. "Only a couple of us work the night shift."

"Is there any shift you don't work?" Fallon asked with a smile. "You seem to always be working. You do sleep, right?" she joked.

Jess grinned. She had strong features, but they softened a lot when she laughed, showing good humor. "Just about every day," she quipped. "I pull a lot of double shifts."

"Right," Fallon said. "You're eager to get off this hunk of metal."

"It's nothing personal," Jess insisted. "I just want to get the job done and go home."

Fallon waved a hand dismissively. "No offense taken. I get it. This is what most people would consider a 'shit assignment.'"

Jess blinked at Fallon's use of a swear word, then laughed in surprise. "Well, you're right about that. Not that the work itself is bad, or the conditions are bad. Just...the isolation makes me uneasy, you know?"

Fallon nodded. "To be honest, I'm eager for the crew to arrive and make this place feel like it isn't a ghost station."

It wasn't exactly a lie. Though Fallon didn't mind the deserted feeling of Asimov, she felt eager to move on to phase two of her assignment there. She was eager to meet Captain Lydecker and start sizing him up.

They fell into step together, heading toward the alpha sector of the station, where most of the major control areas were located.

"So when you go home, where will you be going?" Fallon asked. She hadn't interacted with Jess as much as others in the crew. Now she realized this was mostly due to the woman's workaholic nature.

"Zerellus," Jess answered.

"I seem to remember that you're originally from Earth. Or did I get that wrong?" Fallon knew every word written in Jess' personnel file, of course, but she wanted some safe topics of conversation to establish some rapport.

"That's right," Jess agreed. "I traveled around from place to place, wherever work took me. Of all the places I've been, I liked Zerellus the best, so I decided to make it my home. Of course, when a good opportunity arises. I still have to go to wherever the job happens to be."

"Sounds familiar," Fallon said. "Except for me, home is wherever my assignment is."

"Really?" Jess asked. "You don't have family somewhere, and think of wherever they are as home?"

"Well, I do, in a broader sense." Fallon thought about it. Did she really think of anywhere as home? "But PAC headquarters is my home, I guess. I haven't spent much time on Jamestown yet, but it's where PAC command is, so I guess that's home now, in the more immediate sense."

Jess grinned. "Sounds like you haven't really thought about it before."

"I haven't," Fallon admitted honestly. "I've been focused on being an officer and the future rather than defining my present."

They came to another cross section. Fallon moved left, while Jess moved to the right.

"Looks like this is where we part ways," Jess joked, stopping in place. "Good talking to you."

"You too," Fallon said, trying to match Minho's easy way of talking to people. "Be sure to take some downtime. Don't work yourself into exhaustion."

"No worries," Jess assured her. "I once worked seventy-six hours straight and didn't fall down. A couple months of double shifts is nothing."

They exchanged a casual wave and continued on their individual paths.

As Fallon returned the tool kit to engineering, she pondered the question of home. Jamestown seemed like the right answer in terms of location. She'd sent most of her personal items to Jamestown to go into her storage unit. The few things she'd brought with her to Asimov were only what she needed for the duration of her time there.

What did home mean for her now?

She entered her quarters, got a cup of water, and sat on the floor with her back against the front of the couch.

Earth was her home planet, and where she was from. It was where her parents and brother lived. But she didn't think of it as her home. She felt no pull to return to it, and no deep feelings of missing it.

Wasn't that what she should feel about her home?

Yes, that was it. Home wasn't a place for her anymore. It was a feeling. She drained her water and stood. After setting the cup in the kitchenette, she went to the necessary to shower.

She took her time standing in the steam of the shower. How nice that Asimov had hydro showers rather than the sonic type. The sonic ones might clean the skin, but they sure didn't have the same relaxing qualities of a hydro shower.

The people stationed on Asimov would be lucky to receive such modern conveniences.

As she put her towel in the processor, she remembered Hawk stealing her towels in officer training school. She smiled.

A feeling of fondness and belonging welled up in her, confirming her previous conclusion. Home was not a matter of where she was, but who she was with.

Avian Unit was her home. Everything else was just a way station.

A HIGH-PITCHED ELECTRONIC warble yanked Fallon from sleep. She immediately rolled out of bed and hurried to the nearest voicecom display.

She'd silenced the voicecom for everything but priority calls when she'd gone to bed.

That meant something had gone wrong.

Her blood already pumping, she activated the display. "Arashi here."

Katheryn's scrunched face appeared. "There's a containment breach in section gamma."

"Have you sealed that section off?"

"Yes." The lieutenant seemed tense, but in control.

Fallon nodded. "I'll meet you there. Has Minho checked in?"

"He said exactly the same things you did. Except for the part asking about him, of course."

Fallon nodded again and deactivated the screen.

On her way out of her quarters, she grabbed a bright-yellow bag.

PAC regulations stipulated that all equipment belonging to the station must be returned to its correct location at the end of a shift, but it didn't say anything about officers owning their own emergency tool kits to keep in their quarters.

She slung the bag over her shoulder so that it hung cross-body. It was a decent set of multipurpose tools. If it didn't have what they needed, they'd find the necessary items in an equipment locker in section gamma.

Minho emerged from his quarters just as she passed his door. He had a bright orange bag slung over his shoulder.

"Nice pajamas," she said.

She wasn't kidding. His sapphire-blue pants and long-sleeved shirt had a slight sheen to them, and molded to his form nicely.

He smirked, and they broke into a run. "You too."

She wore a pair of low-rise shorts and a tank top. She was, for certain, showing a whole lot more skin than any officer normally would during her duties, but in the event of a serious emergency, even the dress code became irrelevant.

Minho's long, smooth stride was not only fast, but each step also landed lightly. He was a good runner.

So was she. She increased her pace to edge ahead of him just slightly, holding her tool kit against her chest to keep it from jostling around.

A moment later, he regained a very slight lead.

The gauntlet had been thrown.

She'd already charted a mental path to take the shortest route to the topmost level of the station. Deck 6 housed the largest machinery that made the station habitable, including the containment units. They could run diagnostics from there, then put on containment suits to go repair the problem.

With a mental image of the ship's blueprint in her mind, she estimated that she had half a kilometer between her and the lift that would take them up.

She could easily sprint that distance, so she summoned all the strength in her legs to put on a burst of speed that had her quickly outdistancing Minho.

He just as quickly closed that distance.

She would have grunted in irritation, but she needed all her breath to beat him.

They ran on. Each time they approached a cross section, she sent a fervent wish for no one to pop out and cause a collision.

They turned a corner and she could see the lift ahead. She dug deep for all the speed she had in her body and willed herself to make it there first.

She didn't let up until she had to, unless she wanted to

bash herself right into the doors of the lift. She reached out, both to hasten her arrival and absorb some of her momentum.

Minho's hands touched the doors at the same moment.

"Augh!" she gasped. It didn't come out sounding frustrated, due to her heavy breathing. It sounded more like squawk of a startled little bird.

"Why are you so competitive?" He played it cool, trying to hide his heavy breathing.

He wasn't fooling her.

"What, like I can be competitive all by myself? Like you weren't running as hard as you could?"

"I could have run harder if I wanted to." His hand on his chest and his labored breathing marked his statement as tremendously unlikely.

"Liar," she said.

He gave her a look of mock outrage. "How dare you say that to your superior officer."

"Superior, nothing," she snorted. "So far you haven't managed to beat me at anything."

He fixed her with a stare that, she was pretty sure, was intended to melt her face off.

They both burst out laughing.

The lift doors opened and they hurried in.

Fallon looked pointedly at Minho's tool kit. "I see you planned ahead."

He grinned suddenly, his breathing coming easier now. "Back at you."

"Better safe than sorry, right?"

"Absolutely." He nodded in agreement.

By the time they arrived on Deck 6, they were breathing normally.

"I told Lee to have the crew suit up and meet us up there. Hopefully the repairs won't be extensive." Minho's eyes weren't on her, but on the readout that indicated their arrival at their destination.

They hurried out of the lift and to the nearby location of the deck's main diagnostics. Immediately, they began pulling up information, looking for what went wrong.

"Hang on," Fallon said. "This clearly indicates a broken seal, but the pressure inside is exactly what it should be."

Minho stared intently at the voicecom panel. "Either the pressure indicator is faulty, or the seal sensor is."

"Let's find out which," she said. "If pressure is accurate, I should be able to do a brief exhaust of the air vents and it won't affect the air mix inside."

"Good thought to test," Minho said. "Unless the air filtration sensors are faulty."

"One thing at a time, I guess," she said. "Venting." After a count of three, she turned off the vent. Then she counted to ten and checked the air quality of the sealed-off portion of the deck.

"It's stable. I don't think we have a containment breach."

"Seems unlikely," Minho agreed. "We should have some reinforcements in suits coming any minute, so let's let them go in and confirm."

"You don't want to suit up and do it ourselves?"

He shook his head. "They've gotten a good shakeup. It's good for them to get practice, and they'll feel better if they had some part in all this."

She understood. "It would be a bummer for them to show up here, adrenaline high, only to be told it was nothing and that they should go away."

He nodded. "Exactly. Since there doesn't appear to be a real emergency, it's better to let them handle the situation. Especially for the two who will remain on the station."

They monitored the situation while the minutes ticked by. Seven minutes after Fallon and Minho had arrived, Katheryn, Jess, and Priestley showed up, fully kitted out in pressure suits.

Not bad time at all, considering they had to get into the suits then make their way here in them, which would have slowed their progress a little.

Plus, they all acted as if Minho and Fallon weren't standing there in their jammies. Fallon mentally gave them extra professionalism points for that.

"Good news," Minho told the newcomers. "We're pretty sure we're only looking at a sensor repair. However, it will be up to you three to go in, confirm that containment is solid, and do the repair. Are you up for it?"

Jess and Katheryn nodded immediately, with Priestly following with a quick, not entirely certain nod a moment later.

"Until we know for certain," Minho advised, "proceed with the assumption that containment has been breached. Don't take any unnecessary risks. Do this by the book."

Katheryn led the way around the deck to the emergency airlock into the section. Unlike a regular airlock, it was little more than a tiny buffer zone that could accommodate four people at a time to ensure the sealed region couldn't contaminate the rest of the station.

Fallon and Minho watched the team's progress on the voice-com. The three entered the sealed-off portion of the deck and retrieved equipment from a supply locker.

Within moments, Katheryn reported, "There's no breach. The sensor's indicating one, but everything's fine in here."

Fallon had suspected as much, but relaxed, nonetheless. Even the outside chance of a containment breach was a huge issue—not only from a safety standpoint, but also as a major obstacle in getting the station set up and ready for the rest of the crew to arrive. Most of those people were already in route. A delay caused by a structural failure would have been a major issue.

The three of them worked well at diagnosing the failure and replacing the faulty sensor. Even Priestley performed with a high degree of skill and professionalism, once he got to work.

Katheryn spoke over the voicecom. "Activating the new sensor. Then I'll proceed with an auto-diagnostic cycle to clear the malfunction."

Minho said nothing and simply watched.

The new sensor snapped to life and a moment later, the containment alert prompted a second-level self-diagnostic from the system.

The alert disappeared.

"All systems functioning properly," Katheryn reported, her voice full of satisfaction.

"Very good," Minho said. "You can proceed with unsealing the section. Then begin an investigation into that faulty sensor. Find out if we have more from that batch, and do a manual inspection of all critical sensors. Then log a critical failure for the component with PAC command. They'll follow up with the manufacturer."

"Understood," Katheryn said.

"Good work."

"Thank you." Katheryn's voice was clipped and professional, but obviously pleased.

"Let's go," Minho said.

"We're not going to stay here and supervise?" Fallon asked, surprised.

"Nope. This is their job. Of course, we'll follow up on everything independently to double-check their work, but I think they'll do just fine."

"Hm." Fallon followed him back to the lift, feeling a bit let down.

"Problem?" he asked.

"No. We're lucky not to be dealing with a major problem right now. It's good."

"But you were all set to do something exciting, right? And you're just headed back to your quarters instead." He smiled knowingly.

She rolled a shoulder in a half-shrug. "Adrenaline rush is hard to deny."

"Yeah. But this is the job. False alarms happen. You have to either get used to it, or find a way to work out your excess energy. A good workout can do the trick."

She smiled. "Are you offering some sparring?"

They hadn't done that since arriving on Asimov. She missed their training sessions. She always had a great time when they were trying to cripple each other.

"No," he retorted. "I'm a grown-up with self-control and don't need to work out excess energy. Since my subordinate is so needy, though…I guess I could."

She scoffed. "Don't do me any favors. I can just go for a run or lift some weights."

"What kind of mentor would I be if I relegated you to that?"

She rolled her eyes. "Don't worry about it. I'm good."

He was silent for a moment before saying in a quieter voice, "Well, now that you mention it, a bit of sparring would be good."

She laughed. "You're so transparent."

"Am not," he denied.

"If you were any more transparent, you'd be air."

"Hey," he said, pretending to be offended.

She grinned at him and he grinned back.

Fallon thought of something they'd never competed in. Something she had no doubt she'd win. "So how are you at knife throwing?"

"In my defense," Minho said two hours later, "knife-throwing is not my specialty."

She laughed, pulling knives out of the makeshift target they'd created on the wall in her quarters.

She'd be sure to get that patched up before she left the station.

"Fine," she said. "What's your specialty? We'll compete at that."

"My specialty's axe-throwing," he said.

She looked at him, expecting to see a joking smile, but he looked serious. "Wait...not really, right?"

"Why not?" he asked.

"There's no practical purpose for that."

"Okay. You got me. I'm not a champion axe-thrower," he admitted.

She snorted and returned her set of practice throwing knives to the bandolier she stored them in. "So what's your specialty?"

He put his hands on his hips and leveled a look at her. "I could tell you, but then I'd have to kill you."

She pointed at the door. "Out! Out you go. Good night!"

He smiled. "All right. I'm tired, anyway."

As he passed, he put his hand on her head and ruffled her hair, as he might have done to a child. "Get some rest, Sparky. I expect you to be on-duty at the appointed hour."

"Sparky?" She scrunched up her face.

He shrugged. "Trying it out. Doesn't seem like it fits. Anyway, good night."

She made a *get out* gesture at him and, with another grin, he ducked out of her quarters.

Once he was gone, she permitted herself to smile.

4

After another long day of installing security on Asimov, Fallon met up with Katheryn Lee for a drink in the lieutenant's quarters. It was the first time she'd received such an invitation, so Fallon was curious, even though she was tired from not sleeping much the night before.

"What can I get you?" Katheryn asked when Fallon had taken a seat on the couch in her quarters. Other than being a bit smaller, the space was similar to Fallon's own temporary living situation. The décor was a little more elaborate, with creamy yellow and sage green details.

"I don't know," Fallon said. "What do you have?"

Katheryn returned with three bottles. "Alturian brandy, Zerellian ale, and Terran tequila. My own private stash. I don't often share, so enjoy it while you can."

The lieutenant grinned, then ducked her head, perhaps having second thoughts about her cheeky response.

"I'll have the Terran tequila," Fallon decided. "I like the alliteration."

Katheryn grabbed two cups and returned, sitting down to pour them each a shot of tequila. She lifted her cup. "One shot?"

Fallon shrugged. "Sure, why not?"

They each tossed a shot back, then slammed the cups down on the table, as custom dictated.

"I don't have much in the way of mixers," Katheryn said apologetically. "I was lucky to fit these into my luggage."

"No worries," Fallon assured her. "I grew up in a culture where drinking well is considered a skill. And even if I hadn't, I went to school with a guy who would have made me learn."

She smiled, thinking of Hawk and the fun nights they'd had in his favorite bars. She hoped that, wherever he was, he'd found a watering hole to tide him over.

"A boyfriend?" Katheryn asked with a sly expression.

Fallon laughed. "Oh, no, never. We definitely weren't each other's type for that sort of thing. We were more like best friends and soul mates."

"Ah." Katheryn poured another pair of shots and they downed them. After a pause, she spoke again. "What about you and Minho?"

"What about us?"

"You two seem very well-suited," Katheryn observed.

Fallon shook her head. "We are, but not like that. There's nothing at all romantic going on between us."

"Really?" Katheryn seemed surprised. "You seem perfect for each other."

Fallon sensed that she and Minho had been gossiped about among the crew. And why not? There was little enough on Asimov at present to keep people entertained. Some new blood around the place to fuel speculation was fair game.

"Really," Fallon assured her. "We're just friends and colleagues."

Fallon saw a glint of something in Katheryn's expression, and came to a revelation of her own. "You're interested in him."

Katheryn's cheeks went pink. "Well, who wouldn't be?" She

made a gesture that was probably supposed to appear easygoing, but actually came across as self-conscious.

Fallon decided to let her off the hook. "Sure, he's good-looking and genuinely nice. I imagine he gets a lot of romantic interest."

Katheryn sighed and sank back into the couch cushions. "You're right. He's out of my league."

Fallon chuckled. "I said nothing of the sort. In fact, I don't know anything about what kind of person he likes, so maybe you're exactly his type."

Katheryn perked up slightly. "You think so?"

"Anything's possible."

Katheryn smiled. "You're teasing me."

"My words are sincere. I'm just saying them in a teasing manner because this feels perilously close to girl talk."

Katheryn poured them each a third shot. "There's nothing wrong with girl talk, so long as it isn't mean-spirited. Womanly bonding is important." She nodded for emphasis. "Especially in situations of limited interpersonal contact."

Fallon set her cup on the table. "Uh oh. That sounds like PAC psychological training for deep-space missions."

"I'm the kind of girl who does her homework," Katheryn declared.

Fallon smiled. It hadn't been long since they'd downed their first shots, but Katheryn seemed a little tipsy already. Maybe she'd warmed up with a shot or two before Fallon had arrived. The thought amused her, and made her like Katheryn Lee a little more than she already did.

If the lieutenant was feeling a little more loose-lipped than usual, it might be a good time to probe her about the crew. She'd been with them longer than Fallon had, and might have some insights.

"How has it been, working here all this time? I bet you're ready for the place to be populated."

Katheryn nodded. "I really am. I'm curious to meet the captain, and eager to get to a regular daily schedule."

"And be a command officer for the first time," Fallon added.

"Sure."

"Have any of the set-up crew caused you any trouble?"

Katheryn pursed her lips thoughtfully. "There were a few minor disagreements amongst them in terms of who would work on what, but that got worked out pretty quickly. So no, no real problems."

Fallon nodded slowly and said nothing, letting the silence stretch out and become awkward in the hope that it would prompt Katheryn to keep talking about the crew.

"They all have their positive attributes and their quirks," Katheryn said. "It was just a matter of getting to know them a little to figure out how best to work as a team. I think we do pretty well now, with most people working pretty independently."

"Who's the most independent?" Fallon asked.

"Jess, probably," Katheryn said. "She's very experienced, and sometimes that means she's a little opinionated, but she knows her stuff."

"Does anyone clash with her?"

"No, not now. There were a few misunderstandings at first because people weren't accustomed to her bluntness, but like I said, that kind of thing resolved itself pretty quickly."

"You got lucky, then," Fallon said. "Imagine if you'd had a bunch of big personalities who were quick to take offense."

Katheryn grimaced. "That's a good point. I'll have to send PAC command a thank-you letter for the assignment."

She waited a beat, then they both laughed.

"You know," Fallon said, "I believe Minho likes Zerellian ale. Maybe you should invite him along next time."

"You don't think that would be weird?"

"I think it would be weird if you didn't," Fallon countered. "We're the top three ranking officers here. Officers tend to get pretty tight when they're assigned to a station or some other far-flung location."

"Hm. Okay. We'll do that one night." Katheryn nodded. She seemed stone sober now, so maybe her previous appearance of tipsiness had just been self-consciousness.

"Maybe at the end of the week," Fallon said. "We're doing a hard push to finish installation of the security system. I'm sure we'll be glad to celebrate having that stage done."

Katheryn nodded. "Moving on to diagnostics will be nice. By that point, all parts of the station will be fully operational."

"I love those two words, when put together. They're nice, don't you think?"

Katheryn laughed. "Fully operational? Yeah. It definitely beats the alternative."

Fallon smiled and stood. "Well, thank you for inviting me over and sharing your stash."

"No problem. I have more coming on the next delivery."

"Oh, so you're just being stingy by not sharing with the rest of the crew," Fallon teased.

"Nah." Katheryn took the cups to the kitchenette and returned. "I just know that if I become the source, I will always be the source. No thank you. They can order their own."

"Smart thinking. I like it. See you tomorrow."

"Yep. Sleep well."

Fallon waved before stepping out the door. She went to her quarters, only a short walk down the corridor. Checking the time, she saw that she'd be able to get a nice, long rest that night.

Good. She needed it. Both because she felt a little sleep-deprived, and because the coming week was going to be intensely busy.

"WHERE ARE YOU?" Minho's voice came over Fallon's comport. "I thought we were going to meet at Katheryn's to celebrate completing the installation."

Fallon scooted down a maintenance conduit. "I had some time, so I thought I'd start doing manual checks of all the drones, since that's the next step."

"Well, I hope you're not planning to do them all tonight."

"Hah. Hardly. That wouldn't even be possible. Even after recruiting some of the others to do this, it will still take a couple of days."

"All the more reason for you not to be late today," Minho said.

"Wow, you're not afraid of being alone with her, are you?"

"Of course not. But being alone with her in her quarters... well, I'd rather not. I suspect she has a crush on me."

"You suspect correctly, I think," Fallon said.

"Well, hurry up, then."

She finished checking the security drone installed in this conduit. It was in good order. "Fine. On my way."

"ONE MORE?" Katheryn asked, holding the bottle of Zerellian ale.

"Sure," Fallon said.

Katheryn poured a shot for herself, Fallon, and Minho, and said, "One shot!"

They all downed it.

"This has been fun," Katheryn said. "I hope it's like this when the captain and the rest of the permanent crew arrive."

"I'm sure you'll find people to hang out with—officers and contractors alike," Minho said. "And stations have such a mix of people always arriving and departing that things tend to stay interesting."

"I hope so," Katheryn said. "I've heard some horror stories about being assigned to a space station."

"Ignore them," Minho advised. "People like to tell horror stories. They're fun. They're usually very overexaggerated, too."

"Besides," Fallon added, "this is a big, brand-new station. What I'd worry about is being stuck on some four-person outpost somewhere. Just four people on a tiny bucket in the middle of nowhere for six months?" She grimaced for comedic effect. "No thank you."

"Another good point. Thanks."

"You'll do fine," Minho assured her. "And one day, when you're the captain of one of these things, I'll expect free drinks whenever I pass through."

Fallon and Katheryn laughed.

"Deal," Katheryn promised.

Fallon checked the time. "Yep. Time for me to sleep. I have about a hundred billion drones to check in the next few days."

"A slight exaggeration," Minho said dryly. "And there will be four others of us doing the same thing, so don't expect too much sympathy."

"I never do." She smiled at Katheryn. "See you tomorrow."

Minho said his goodbye and hurried out into the corridor, practically on Fallon's heels. "I can't believe you almost left me in there," he hissed under his breath.

"I felt like you could handle her."

"Hah." He did not sound amused.

"You don't like her, even a little?" Fallon asked.

They arrived at her quarters and Minho pointed, indicating he'd come in for a minute. When the doors closed behind him, he said, "The lieutenant is a capable officer, nice-looking, and pleasant to hang out with. But I could never date someone who wasn't in Blackout. They just wouldn't understand who I really am, and the lies. I'd have to tell so many lies to someone I supposedly cared about. How could that possibly work?"

She'd been mostly teasing, but he'd gone and gotten super serious all of a sudden. It was an interesting topic, though, and one they hadn't touched on before, even when she'd talked to him about her relationship with Raptor.

"I guess I never thought about it that way," she said. She hadn't had any reason to, since the person she cared about was already in Blackout.

"Most Blackout officers don't have serious relationships. They have flings and short-term things. Our lifestyle doesn't lend itself to domestic bliss or growing old together."

"That's grim," she said.

"What we do is grim." He shrugged. "You're still new. You'll see. The longer you do this, the more the concept of serious romantic entanglement will seem..." he paused, searching for the right word. "Inapplicable."

She gave him a long look. "So what you're saying is that you like Sarkavians."

The people of Sarkan had a much more relaxed approach to relationships than most people from other planets. Monogamy was uncommon there, while open-ended relationships were the norm.

He shook his head at her in exasperation. "You think you're funny, don't you?"

"Sometimes," she admitted, stepping forward to activate the doors to her quarters, which swished open. "Now go. Goodnight!"

He muttered something in response, and she suspected it was at least somewhat unflattering to her.

She laughed as she walked to the necessary to get ready for bed.

"TWENTY THOUSAND, two hundred and fifty-eight drones done, and one to go." Fallon crawled down the conduit for her last drone check. Her running count of how many of them she'd already checked was fiction rather than reality, but it felt like the truth.

When she had made sure the last drone was fully functional, she rewarded herself by lying back in the conduit, closing her eyes, and letting out a long sigh.

She spent a few minutes just listening to the stillness inside the bowels of the station. It was nice. Calming, really. Having spent so much time in them, she could imagine taking a nap in one.

She tucked the idea away, just in case there was some time in her life that she wanted to sleep without being found.

Amused, she got back up and started on her way out of the conduit.

When she climbed out, she closed it behind her and indulged in a good back and arm stretch. At least these general-access conduits were a little larger than the ones that were locked down for security purposes, but she could use a good massage or about an hour lying on a techbed to work out her kinked muscles.

Surely the infirmary already had the techbeds installed and in full operation. She'd have to check that out.

At least her tool kit was of the common variety that could be found at regular intervals around the station. She wouldn't have to trek it all the way back to main engineering or some other place in the opposite direction of her quarters.

After securing the tools and logging them in, she paused to consider which she wanted more—a soothing session on a techbed or food. It was a tough call.

If she grabbed some food first, she'd enjoy the techbed more. *Fine. Decision made.*

The makeshift mess hall was closer than her quarters, so she went there first. Opening cabinets and the cooler, she tried to decide what she could prepare soonest and consume quickest.

Noodle soup seemed like her best bet. One heat-ex setting and two minutes of her time would enable her to slurp down the noodles and soup. That would be enough to tide her over until after her techbed session.

She'd enjoy a snack at a more leisurely pace afterward.

They were simple goals, but sometimes, happiness was a very simple thing.

As she ate, she checked her comport to see if the specialized techbeds in the locker rooms of the station's gym were fully operational.

Success.

Those were specifically designed for user-friendly service after overusing one's body. Exactly what she needed.

After cleaning her dishes and putting them away, she grabbed a protein bar. On the way to the gym, she ate it.

By the time she arrived at the gym, the food had taken the edge off her hunger. In retrospect, she should have brought a second protein bar and eaten it while she was on the techbed, but it was too late for that now.

She entered and walked directly across the gym toward the lockers. It was only when she was halfway across that she noticed someone up on the track, running. After a careful look, she realized it was Priestley. He didn't appear to notice her.

Too bad he didn't have someone to run with. Having a partner always made it more challenging and enjoyable.

Asimov had a nice gym. An enclosed pegball court was off at the far end, and she also saw a large climbing wall, a boxing ring, and multiple cardio and weight machines. Once the crew arrived, it would be up to them to initialize all the equipment and get everything into working order, but it was all there, waiting to be put to use.

Just like the rest of the station.

Soon. In only two more weeks, this place would be buzzing with life. She had a lot to do before then, too.

But for now, she'd take a little time to rest and get herself in shape for the next day.

She passed by the rows of lockers to the back of the locker room. A single techbed had been installed, and waited for her command.

Gym-style techbeds like this had very little in common with medical-grade ones. Physically, they looked mostly the same, but this unit was very simple compared to the kind that doctors used in an infirmary.

She lay down and let the machine scan her, looking for inflammation, swelling, bruising, misalignment, and other minor issues. Any notable injuries would prompt an alert to seek medical treatment.

Fortunately, she didn't need a professional's help. She'd have been out of luck, since the medical crew hadn't arrived yet.

For some reason, she found that funny and chuckled as the techbed worked its magic.

A half hour later, her sore muscles had been soothed and she felt renewed. If not for her general fatigue, she could do another work shift.

She wondered if Jess utilized the techbed to continue with her double shifts.

She probably did.

As she walked through the gym, she looked for Priestley, but he'd already left. She made a mental note to check up on him and make sure he was doing okay.

Approaching the exit, she thought about what she wanted to do with her evening. She felt like doing something quiet in her quarters. A holo-vid, maybe, or doing some language study.

The doors opened just before she reached the sensor and Jacen Arrem froze to avoid walking into her path.

"Sorry, Emiko. I didn't expect anyone to be here, and I was just barreling along."

"Not at all. We didn't even bump into each other." She smiled to put him at ease.

"Getting a workout?" he asked. "It's a nice gym."

"It is, but no. Just a visit to the techbed to ease my back. I had a bit of hunchback syndrome, with all the upper and lower back pain that goes with it."

"Ahh." He nodded sympathetically. "I know it well."

"You just barely missed Priestley," she said. "He was running earlier. Maybe you two could coordinate and work out together."

Jacen nodded. "I'll check with him, thanks. That guy's too shy for his own good. He must be lonely."

"Could be. But you guys have things in common. You're both young, are on this station, and have legs...so why not work out together?"

He laughed. "I'll use that when I try to convince him to come with me."

"Don't blame me if you do and it doesn't work." She chuckled.

"I promise I won't."

"I'll leave you to it," she said. "Enjoy!"

"You bet." He moved aside and walked past her into the gym.

She strolled back to her quarters at a leisurely pace. After all the rushing around she'd been doing, she was in the mood to take things slowly and center herself in calmness.

It seemed like a good way to transition into the last preparations of Asimov, and think ahead toward the investigation of Captain Lydecker.

As she walked through the corridor, she imagined it full of life, with crew members bustling this way and that way. She liked that thought. She felt good about helping to put Asimov into service.

It was nice to feel useful, like she was finally doing something good for the PAC.

She arrived at her quarters and went to the kitchenette. She put her voicecom into do-not-disturb until morning so that anyone intending to invite her to something would see that she was occupied. Then she put together a simple meal of chicken, rice, and a salad.

Her food prep skills were improving, thanks to Minho.

After they were done here and she reunited with Avian Unit, would he continue as a mentor for the team, or would he be given a new assignment? If he knew, he'd never mentioned it, and she'd never asked. Most likely, PAC command would send him to some new position, but she wished he could become a member of her team for real, rather than just honorarily. He had experience, a different skillset than the rest of them, and got along well with all of them.

If she requested he be added to her team, would PAC command even consider it? Would Minho?

It would be beyond presumptuous for her to make such a request.

On the other hand…she was the team leader of a Blackout unit. Wasn't it her job to look out for the best interests of the team? They'd certainly be stronger with Minho.

Before she had a chance to second-guess herself, she left her food in the kitchenette and sat down at the voicecom. She opened a channel to Admiral Krazinski, ensured it was secure, then paused. Normally, she'd communicate via an image feed, but a request like this felt like it should be more formal.

Yes, she'd make it a written request.

She let out a deep breath, staved off the voice that told her to reconsider this, and began speaking.

"Admiral Krazinski, as the team leader of my unit, it is my duty to ensure the team's maximum efficiency. To that end, I formally request that our current mentor be added as an official member of the team, in whatever capacity you and he deem appropriate."

Should she say more? Justify her reasoning?

No. Krazinski would know all possible arguments both for and against the placement. Best to keep it simple. As per protocol, she didn't mention any names but the admiral's in the message, so it felt a little vague for something so significant, but there was no way around that.

Fine. She should just do it, before she changed her mind.

Her hand hovered over the voicecom.

Delete or send?

She was hesitating too long. Giving herself too much opportunity for second thoughts.

"Send message," she said quickly.

It was done. She grimaced, wondering if she'd just made a big mistake or a massive faux pas.

Well, there was nothing to do about it now. Most likely, Krazinski would either assign Minho to the team, if that fit with his plans, or, more likely, simply ignore her request.

She'd just have to wait and see.

After retrieving her still-hot food from the kitchenette, she sat down in front of the couch. She used the low table in front of the couch as a table. It reminded her of living with her parents in Japan, and sitting on the floor at a low table rather than a high table with chairs.

Rather than turn on a holo-vid or some music, she listened to silence as she ate. At least, as silent as life got on a space station. It seemed like silence until she really started to pay attention to her surroundings.

Space stations and ships both had a certain, barely perceptible hum. She couldn't explain it, but it was there—not quite a sound, not quite a vibration. A sort of resonance. Of course, ships and space stations had very different feels. Ships in motion had a more obvious sense of sound and vibration. The feel of a space station was far subtler.

Look at her now! Once a largely Earth-bound girl, she was now a space-dweller. A senior officer, even.

It was hard not to feel good about that. She hadn't even had her twenty-second birthday yet.

She tried to imagine herself at age thirty, and what she might have accomplished by then. No luck. She really couldn't imagine that far into her future.

Once she'd finished eating, she set her dishes aside and exhaled slowly, letting her head fall back. She soaked in the sense of stillness and quiet.

The door chime rang, bringing her head up. She'd forgotten to set it to do-not-disturb mode.

Ah well. At least she'd had a little solitude.

"Doors open," she said aloud as she stood. She didn't usually use voice commands for environmental controls, but sometimes they were more convenient than proximity sensors.

Minho stood in the corridor, looking curious. "Anything wrong?"

He stepped in and the doors closed behind him.

"No," she assured him. "Just giving myself a little victory lap after completing the installation. You know, a quiet evening. Alone."

She arched an eyebrow at him pointedly.

"Ah. Gotcha. Sorry. I just wanted to check up on you, since it's unusual for you to go all do-not-disturb. I thought maybe you'd gotten cabin fever and decided to start plotting something nefarious."

"Like what?" she asked.

"I don't know," he admitted. "But I'm sure it would be terrible."

He grinned, and the corners of his eyes crinkled up in that charming way that they did.

She settled back into her previous spot and gestured at the couch. "Have a seat."

"I don't want to intrude."

His politeness made her smile.

"What?" he asked.

"I was just thinking how much more courteous you are than

my teammates. When you want to be, anyway. If Hawk wanted to be here, there would be very little I could do to get him out."

"Yes, well. Not everyone can be this ideal." He put a hand on his hip and tilted his head back, affecting a pompous expression. "I know it's unfair to everyone else."

She smirked. "Hah. Your sense of humor fits right in, though. Actually, you're a great fit for the team."

He dropped the act and sent her a curious look. "I feel like you're leading up to something."

She gestured to the couch again. "First, sit. You're being weird, towering about over there."

He sat. "I don't tower."

"You do."

He shook his head. "Fine. So what were you saying before?"

"I was just wondering," she paused, suddenly feeling self-conscious. What if the idea of being on her team offended him? He'd had a team. He might not want to revisit all that. "You know, since you fit with Avian Unit so well, if you'd consider a long-term assignment with us."

"I go wherever Blackout tells me to. I don't pick my assignments."

"Of course not," she said quickly. "But if you could, would you want to?"

"Since I've been with you pretty long-term already, I'm guessing you actually mean something more like 'indefinitely.' Is that right?"

She shrugged, going for a casual vibe. "Sure. Hypothetically speaking."

"Now you're the one being weird," he said. "But I'll play along. If I were assigned as a long-term associate of Avian Unit, I wouldn't hate it."

"Prelin's ass," she swore. "Have you ever heard the phrase, 'damned by faint praise?' You're about to hurt my feelings, here."

He grinned. "Look at you, swearing like a grown-up. Aw."

"And now you're antagonizing me again, like when we first met. I take it back. You're not polite and I rescind my invitation. Avian Unit is now officially a no-Minhos-allowed club." She crossed her arms.

"Oh, so it's a full-on invitation? Not just a hypothetical?" He was enjoying this too much.

"Nope," she denied. "You're far too obnoxious to invite into my super-secret club. I already have a Hawk, so we're full up on obnoxiousness, with no vacancies. Sorry."

He laughed. "If I got orders to be part of Avian Unit, I'd be glad. How's that?"

She squinted at him, looking for any hints of teasing, but his smile seemed only warm and sincere.

He was really good at switching between sincerity and sarcasm. She needed to up her game, apparently.

"Too bad you're not invited," she said.

"Maybe I should make a special request." He rubbed his chin thoughtfully.

"Would Krazinski grant it?" she asked.

"Only if it was in line with his long-term plans. And there's no telling what those are. The man plays the long game like no one else in the galaxy."

"Hm." That didn't give her any insight into whether Krazinski would consider her request or not.

He shifted his weight, preparing to stand. "I should go. You wanted to be alone."

"I did. But I had some quality me time. You can stick around if you want to."

"All right." He kicked off his shoes and propped his feet on the table. "So what are we doing tonight?"

She laughed. He switched gears quickly. "How about a holo-vid and some snacks?"

He sat up straighter. "You have snacks? Don't tease me."

"I brought a few favorites with me," she admitted. "I might even share, if you promise not to throw things at the vid."

"Aw. That's one of the best things about watching a vid. But okay. For you, and for snacks, I will compromise." He put on a long-suffering expression.

"Fine. I'll get the snacks. You get the drinks."

He stood. "Actually, I have some chocolate candy. I'll go get it, then grab the drinks."

"Chocolate? You've been holding out all this time."

He winked at her before heading for the door.

She smiled as she opened the cabinet. If she weren't already fully invested in Raptor, it would have been easy to fall for Minho.

5

Katheryn gasped, and her face flushed bright red. "Oh no! I thought I had it that time."

She gazed in despair at the drone she'd smashed into the hull. It lay there in a sad, deactivated lump, with one propeller bent. "I don't know if I'll get this."

"You will," Fallon assured her. "Drone piloting isn't easy. You don't even have a flight rating, which all security officers do, so you're starting from zero. You'll get there."

Katheryn picked up the drone, which had automatically deactivated when it impacted the bulkhead, and grimaced. "Thanks, Emiko. But look, I damaged it."

"All the better for you to learn how to replace a prop," Fallon said. "Seriously, don't worry about it. You'll do most of your training via simulator. I just like to start with the real thing so you can really imagine it when you're doing the simulator."

"At least I won't be able to do much damage on a simulator." Katheryn smiled self-deprecatingly.

"Like I said, you'll get it. As part of the command crew, you should have basic drone piloting skills. It's something you can work on in your off time. A lot of people find it fun."

"Do you?" Katheryn asked.

"I love flying anything." Fallon chuckled. She always felt most alive when she was flying or fighting. That was probably why she liked both so well.

"I'll work at it," Katheryn said resolutely.

"I'm certain you will." Fallon had no doubts about Katheryn's dedication to her career. "Now grab that repair kit and I'll show you how to change out the props."

After her early-morning sessions with the lieutenant, Fallon moved on to the main part of her day—surveying the entire station via drone, checking every single security component.

It would take every bit of the two weeks she had left before the captain and the rest of the crew arrived, even with Minho's help.

She didn't expect to sleep much in the coming days.

Fallon and Minho set up a schedule where they met in the morning, put on their VR gear, and scanned the station. Although they were technically in the same room for most of each day, they saw each other very little. Instead, they inspected every nook and cranny of the station from their remote location, but in even more detail than they'd be able to see with their own eyes. They checked all heat and radiation emissions, observed power draw, and ensured that everything in the security system worked exactly as it should.

Neither of them wanted to report to the captain, upon his arrival, that the station's security hadn't been completed. Suspected of smuggling or not, Captain Lydecker was a Planetary Alliance Cooperative captain. Not just any other captain, either—a space station captain. The position was generally regarded as being one step away from the admiralty.

Until they had proof that the man was a smuggler, he deserved a whole lot of respect.

The dichotomy between the prestige of his position and her assignment to investigate him did not escape her. In effect, she had a position of authority over someone who far outranked her.

She truly existed in a dark, elite place now. It didn't weigh on her, though. She reveled in it. Finally, she was about to really begin what she had waited so long to do.

Be a clandestine operative. For real.

Fallon threw herself into a grueling schedule of surveying the security system. Minho helped when he had time, but he also oversaw the checks of the other systems. With no other drone pilots currently on board, she had a lot of area to cover.

She set alerts to remind her to eat at regular intervals. She also made sure she slept a full eight hours each day. Other than eating and sleeping, though, she worked almost nonstop. Even when she slept, she dreamed of being in VR, seeing everything as the drone saw it.

After the fourth long day, she removed her VR headgear with a sigh. Smoothing her hair, she decided to visit the mess hall for a snack before she went to bed. Mostly, she wanted the little bit of exercise the walk would provide. She didn't care for being so sedentary for so many days in a row.

She doubted anyone would be in the mess hall. Everyone was now working irregular schedules, staggering or coordinating their shifts to ensure the work was done as efficiently as possible.

When she arrived, though, she found both Priestley and Jacen eating sandwiches.

"Hey, Emiko," Jacen said, as Priestley waved at her in lieu of greeting, indicating his mouth, which was full of food.

"Hi, guys. It's a nice surprise to run into you. I thought I'd be on my own."

Priestley swallowed and said, "We just finished checks on the air containment system. Thought we'd celebrate with some food."

"Good work," she said. "One more system checked off the list, right?"

"Yeah," Jacen agreed. "Though tomorrow we start with the waste treatment checks, so it'll be the same thing with different details."

She smiled, opening a packet of mixed fruit and sitting down with them.

"We're in the home stretch," she said.

"The home what?" Priestley peered at her quizzically.

"It's an Earth phrase. Kind of an old one, I guess. It means we're about to finish the race."

"Ah." Priestley nodded.

"I knew that," Jacen said in a jokingly know-it-all fashion.

"You're from Earth," Priestley pointed out. "I grew up on Zerellus."

"Really?" Jacen squinted at him. "But you look so human."

"Ha ha," Priestley said dryly.

"That's okay," Jacen continued magnanimously. "I don't mind that you're a colonist."

"I think," Priestley said, "that after the first few hundred years, a planet starts being its own thing, rather than a colony."

Fallon simply ate her fruit and smiled, enjoying their friendly taunts. The jokes about Zerellians still being colonists or not being human were old standbys in the pretend rivalry between the two planets.

As were the jokes about Terrans living in caves and cooking by campfire.

"Zerellians are just former Terrans who were smarter than the rest," Priestley said, "and they knew enough to leave."

Another old standby.

"You're from Earth, right, Lieutenant?" Jacen asked casually.

Priestley and Fallon laughed at his attempt to draw her into the debate.

"Yes," she said, "but I consider myself a citizen of the galaxy. Don't look at me to help you out with this one."

Jacen grinned at her. "Scrap. I thought I had an ally."

"I hear Zerellus is actually terrific," Fallon said. "After their colonial days, they established a population with almost no poverty and far lower crime rates than on Earth."

"Maybe that's part of the intelligence thing I said before," Priestley said. His tone wasn't as cheerful or joking now, though. It had an edge to it. "But 'low poverty' doesn't mean 'no poverty.' It just means that the few unlucky ones have a much bigger step down from how the average person lives."

He clearly spoke from experience. It explained why he was so eager to take an undesirable job for the benefit of a long-term position.

"I'm sorry to hear that," Fallon said sincerely. "The PAC isn't perfect yet. Hopefully we can keep working toward the goal of eliminating all poverty on all of our member planets."

Priestley stared down at the remains of his sandwich. She guessed that he regretted saying anything about it.

He nodded, not looking up. He clearly regretted speaking about his circumstances.

Time for a change of subject. "Do either of you have anything you've personally ordered coming on next week's supply delivery?"

Given the impending influx of crew, they'd be onboarding a massive shipment of supplies. They'd receive hygiene products, medical supplies, and most of all, food. Tons and tons of it. Literally.

Plus, of course, crew could get their personal shopping lists fulfilled—like Katheryn refilling her liquor cabinet.

Priestley shook his head. "There's nothing I particularly need. The restaurants and stores will set up soon after the crew arrives, so whatever I end up needing, I'll be able to get there."

Jacen said, "I spent too much money on stocking up my kitchenette. I'll probably have to store some of it in my bedroom."

Priestley squinted at him. "You can't possibly eat all that before you ship out."

Jacen ducked his head, embarrassed. "I know. I just got so excited about the possibility of some added variety that I went a little crazy."

Fallon chuckled. "If you don't want to buy extra luggage to take it all with you, you can always gift it to the people permanently stationed here. I'm sure it would earn you some friends."

"Eh, who needs friends when I have a surplus of food?" Jacen joked.

Fallon finished eating, but remained seated while the men ate. She was about to make polite conversation about Jacen's next assignment when Jess arrived.

"Oh, look at that," the woman said. "A whole crowd getting a late-night snack."

Fallon hadn't crossed paths with Jess for a few days. "If you call three people a crowd. But if you're expecting to see an empty room, it could seem that way. Good to see you."

Jess gave her a little wave of acknowledgement and opened the cooler to survey her options.

"Of the four of us," Fallon said, her eyes on Priestley, "you're the only one who will remain on Asimov. I bet you're looking forward to meeting the captain and other officers."

Priestley shifted, looking ambivalent. "In a way. I mean, I'm curious."

"But probably a little nervous too," Fallon said sympathetically. "You always have to hope the people in charge won't be massive jerks, right?"

Jacen laughed in surprise, and after a moment, Priestley chuckled too.

"Not that I'd ever say that out loud to anyone, but yeah," he admitted.

"Not me," Jess declared, sitting down with a tray of food. She'd prepared a whole meal rather than just a snack. "If I don't like someone, I don't mind saying it. And I'm not one to talk behind people's backs. I'll say it right to them. I don't care if they're officers or whatever. Like they say where I'm from, sour is sour."

"Which means?" Jacen prompted.

Jess stirred her food with her chopsticks. "If something's bad, there's no sense in dressing it up or pretending it's better than it is."

"I like that," Jacen said. "Not having to guess where you stand with someone. I'd rather that than someone who thinks one thing and says another."

The irony of him saying that in Fallon's presence didn't escape her.

"Who has time for that scrap?" Jess asked before taking a bite of a breadstick.

"Well, I do," Fallon admitted. "I can't exactly go around telling senior officers that I think they're cretins, even if they are."

Jess grinned as she chewed. "The chains of command like to keep you tied up, don't they?"

"A hazard of the job," Fallon admitted. "Fortunately, it hasn't really been an issue for me yet. There have been officers that I've liked a lot more than others, but so far I haven't met any that are really terrible."

"You will," Jess said between bites. "Trust me. I've been working around the top brass, the middle brass, and the barely even metal for decades. There are some real shitmeisters out there."

Fallon laughed at the word, which was a new one to her. "Is that a common phrase where you come from?"

"Nah," Jess said. "That's my own invention. Feel free to use it."

"Uh, sure, I'll watch for a good opportunity." Fallon smiled. She was starting to like Jess. Her bluntness reminded her of Peregrine, even though Per was much more private with her thoughts.

Fallon covered a sudden yawn. "Oof. I think that's it for me. I need to get some sleep before I get back to work. It was nice to run into you three. I expected to be all by my lonesome."

"Good to see you," Priestley said.

Jacen nodded and smiled.

Jess just waved distractedly, focusing her attentions on her food like it was a critical mission.

"If any of you come up against anything during this last hard push, be sure to let Minho know," she said.

She ducked out in the direction of her quarters. She should check in with Minho, but she was just too tired. The space between her and her bed seemed to be stretching rather than closing.

By the time she got to her quarters, she'd given up all thoughts of showering or anything else. She fell into bed, reminding herself to check in with Minho first thing in the morning.

"I don't think I've ever seen so much stuff in my life," Katheryn said, watching the delivery crew take hover cart after hover cart out of the docking bay and off to other parts of the station.

"It's supposed to take them a full three days to unload everything," Minho said, standing off to one side with Fallon and Katheryn to stay out of the way of the workers.

"Is that ice cream?" Fallon wondered, watching a cart of frozen items go by. "I think it is."

Minho looked at her with amusement. "Do you need ice cream?"

"Not need," she said. "But when is it ever unwelcome?"

"Good point." He pointed at another cart. "I think that one's medical. It looks like they're doing multiple departments at once. Makes sense. It wouldn't be efficient for them to all go down the same corridors and wait on the same lifts."

"I'm sure the entire delivery was designed with maximum efficiency in mind," Katheryn said.

"Even so," Minho said, "those of us still working on the station itself may find all this activity to be a disruption. If you hear of any issues, be sure to let me know right away. For the most part, we should accommodate the delivery as much as possible. They'll be out of our way in three days."

"Understood," Katheryn said. "Now, as much as I'd like to stay here and keep watching, I need to go see to our people."

"You're doing a good job," Minho said. "Keep it up."

Katheryn blinked in surprise, then smiled. She gave him a small bow of thanks before hurrying off to her day's work.

"How's your part going?" Minho asked.

"I expect to be done in three days. That will give us another three days to handle anything else that needs handling before the captain arrives." She added, "Those three days are also padding, in case anything comes up in my checks."

"Anything significant so far?"

"I've replaced a few power circuits due to readings that were too low for new components. But that's normal. Some circuits just don't last as long as others."

"I have to admit," Minho said, "I'm looking forward to restarting the chronometers when the captain arrives. It's kind of silly symbolism, but it will be cool to be here when the order is given to officially put the station into service."

"I think it will be a satisfying moment," Fallon said. "This station will be here long after we're gone. After the grandchildren of our generation are gone, even. It will be cool to be a part of history in some small way."

"Exactly," he agreed.

"Have you been present at other moments like that?" she asked.

"I could tell you," he began.

She cut him off before he could say he'd have to kill her. "Yep. Catch you later."

Hastily, she made an exit, pleased that she'd prevented him from delivering that line again.

Fallon finished the last check on the last sensor on the last section of the station's outer hull.

Done.

Finished.

After piloting the drone back to its compartment on the side of the station and securing it, she pulled off her VR headgear, sat back, and let out a long, deep sigh.

There. She was as certain as anyone could be that Asimov Station had a fully functioning security system. She'd checked every surveillance angle to make sure there were no dead spots. She'd ensured that redundant systems were all operating as they should, to ensure that no lapses were possible.

She'd done it.

She almost couldn't believe she'd pulled it off. Such a massive project. She'd only had Minho's help, and some assistance from techs when doing the late-stage checks. But they'd gotten it done.

Rubbing her hands over her face, she checked the time. She had four hours until the dinner hour. She didn't know if anyone would show up, given that they were all racing to finish their tasks too, but she'd have dinner at the appointed hour, just in case.

That gave her four hours of time to herself.

She decided to celebrate.

In her kitchenette, she'd stowed a single-serving can of champagne that Katheryn had given her. Fallon didn't know if canned champagne could possibly be any good, but she decided that now was the time to find out.

She cracked the can open and took a sip.

Ugh.

Pulling a cup out of the cabinet, she poured in a finger's worth of tango fruit juice, then layered the champagne over it.

Much better.

She drained the cup, then refilled it the same way.

The second time, she sipped slowly. Sinking into the couch cushions, she considered what to do next.

She felt like doing something indulgent.

Options were, of course, limited. She didn't have to think about it for very long.

After more than a week of being mostly sedentary, some intensely physical activity sounded wonderful.

Tilting her head back, she drained her cup.

After changing into workout wear, she headed for the gym.

Once there, she paused, taking in a deep breath. A gym usually had a certain scent, even with the most aggressive air scrubbers. It wasn't an unpleasant smell by any means, and she kind of missed it. Asimov's gym was too new to have the faint aroma of thousands of workouts pounded into it.

No matter. She'd give it a head start.

Starting up on the track, she ran three kilometers, then attacked the climbing wall.

There was nothing like a good climb for a full-body workout. There was a mental component to it as well, searching for the right combination of grips and footholds. She liked climbing. She hadn't done a great deal of it previously, but she enjoyed the feeling of solving the puzzle of getting to the top.

Once she arrived, she sat on a ledge, looking out at the gym. Soon, it would be full of people. She looked forward to that.

Of course, when there were others around, she'd have to wear the proper safety equipment, which she'd ignored just for today, during her little celebration.

Climbing wouldn't be as fun without the risk of falling.

She smiled, remembering Raptor teasing her about her adrenaline issues. She couldn't help it that she felt most alive when she was fighting or flying. That was why she did those things—to escape the thrum of mediocrity.

Being with her team felt that way, too.

There was a reason she'd chosen this life.

She chose a challenging path down, often relying solely on her upper body strength as she shifted from hold to hold. She sent a mental thank-you to Ross Whelkin for forcing her to increase her muscle mass during the academy. Her slight frame made adding bulk extremely difficult, and she guarded every ounce of muscle zealously.

Once on the ground, she took three running steps, then went into a tumbling run. Handspring, twisting handspring, and a back handspring, ending with a layout back tuck.

She wasn't a gymnast. She wouldn't have scored any points with any judges of the sport. Her movements were to gain distance and put her in a position to strike as soon as she landed, rather than for ideal form.

She loved flips, though. She launched into a cartwheel that gave her plenty of momentum to do her favorite side flip. It was a tricky maneuver. Showy, and not actually very useful in a combat situation, but fun. By throwing her momentum over her shoulder, she could quickly tuck her knees up, almost under her armpits, but successively, allowing her to execute a lateral flip that was not only fun, but tended to impress people.

It had sure impressed Raptor, when she'd first met him. Back then, she'd known him as Drew.

The memory made her smile.

Knowing that she'd accomplished half her assignment, and was that much closer to reuniting with him, Peregrine, and Hawk, made her smile even more.

She was feeling pretty good, and it wasn't the champagne.

Well, it wasn't *just* the champagne. Having grown up drinking sake and makgeolli at the ever-present social occasions of her homeland, she'd never been a lightweight in the drinking department.

A shame she didn't have a sparring partner. She felt remarkably in the mood for a good fight. Minho undoubtedly had better things to do, though, so she did several more tumbling passes, spent some time punching and kicking a training dummy, and ran a few more kilometers.

Finally, when her muscles felt fully released from her recent stint of inactivity, and her entire body felt alive and sweaty, she hit the locker room to shower and dress in a fresh uniform.

Minho had decreed that while the delivery crew was on board, all officers must be in uniform, per standard protocol, whenever they were in view of others. Whether or not he was her friend and partner, he was still the ranking officer on this station, and she accepted the order as she would from any other superior officer.

"Ahhhh!" She stretched her arms with satisfaction as she left, her bag with her other clothes over her shoulder.

Her body felt good. Her mind felt more relaxed. What now? She checked the time. She still had an hour and a half before dinner.

A nap? That sure sounded indulgent. But, having cut some corners on her sleep lately, she did feel tired. Some sleep would not only be pleasant, but also prepare her to jump back into work tomorrow.

Right. She adjusted the strap on her shoulder. A nap it was, then.

6

"READY?" Minho asked in a low voice.

Fallon nodded, her eyes on the airlock. "Ready."

This was it. Her first official transfer of command. Being that it was the official beginning of Asimov Station's service, it felt like a major event.

The airlock opened.

Captain Phillip Lydecker stepped onto Asimov, looking serious and dignified. A Zerellian of forty-six years, standardized to the Terran year, as per PAC tradition, Lydecker looked every bit the senior officer.

Minho stepped up and bowed low, as befitting their difference in rank and the official nature of this meeting. "Lieutenant Commander Minho Park, Captain. Does this command meet your satisfaction?"

It was an age-old question, steeped in ceremony and tradition. It wasn't actually a question, but an acknowledgement of the commanding officer's arrival and an invitation to take his rightful command.

Fallon looked forward to the day when she would be the senior officer being asked that question.

Someday.

"It does," Lydecker confirmed. "Lieutenant Commander Park, you are relieved of this command."

Minho bowed again, but shallowly this time, and took a small step backward.

Heedless of the crew members arriving behind him via the airlock, Captain Lydecker focused his attention on the skeleton crew.

Fallon looked at them, too, all assembled together, solemn but proud of the work they'd done. Even Jess had a certain set in her shoulders that indicated pride and satisfaction.

This might be the last time all of them were together, since everyone but Priestley and Katheryn had already scheduled various transports off the station, and would be departing over the next couple of weeks as those transports arrived to carry them off to their next assignments.

It felt surprisingly bittersweet.

"I am Captain Phillip Lydecker. I formally take command of this station. Asimov Station is, as of this moment, officially registered as a commissioned station of the Planetary Alliance Cooperative."

Discretely, Fallon touched her comport, resetting the station's internal chronometers to mark that precise moment as zero hours, zero minutes, and one second, on day one of its service.

Wow. By her hand, a space station was born. She felt a thrilling rush not unlike the sensation of winning a good fight.

Maybe even a little better.

Actually, she felt a little giddy.

"As your captain," Lydecker continued, "I consider each and every one of you my personal responsibility. I thank you for your diligent attention in preparing Asimov Station for service."

He bowed then, just deeply enough to show respect.

Light applause filled the docking bay and everyone loosened up, with the formalities now out of the way.

"Park Minho." Lydecker approached and bowed to Minho. "I've heard many good things about you. I'm fortunate to have had you overseeing operations here."

Fallon was impressed. Few people, even among PAC officers, would think to put Minho's family name first, as was tradition where he and Fallon were from.

"It was my honor, sir." Minho returned the bow, more deeply.

Lydecker turned to Fallon. "And you must be Arashi Emiko. Thank you for your service. I'm certain we will work well together over the coming weeks."

She bowed. "Thank you, sir. I promise to do my best."

He moved on, greeting those who had served Asimov in order of rank. Priestley, of course, would come last.

Meanwhile, other officers arrived to introduce themselves. First, a few lieutenant commanders, then several lieutenants, then a plethora of ensigns followed by an onslaught of contractors.

Each step down in rank abbreviated the introductions, until the contractors simply walked by, making eye contact and perhaps nodding respectfully.

After Lydecker had made his rounds, Minho and Katheryn went with him to give him the official tour of the station. Fallon remained behind to greet the entirety of the incoming crew.

Two hours later, she was exhausted. Such formal manners in a heightened atmosphere, as it turned out, got tiring quickly. By the end, the others of the skeleton crew had long since disappeared.

It was the benefit of not being an officer, she supposed. She, on the other hand, would be spending her day finding crew members and making personal introductions.

Jess's words came back to her. Jess had been right. The chains of command did pull tight sometimes.

AFTER THE FIRST DAY, a reception breakfast was arranged by the new crew.

A reception breakfast? Was that even a thing?

Apparently so, because they'd clearly had this pre-planned.

Fallon attended, re-greeted the new crew, ate eggs and toast, and engaged in polite small talk.

It wasn't as dreary as the crew's initial arrival on the station, but it required a great deal of vigilance to interact with these officers, maintain her cover identity, and covertly observe the interactions of the people at the gathering.

She'd already made the mental switch to the second part of her assignment, and wanted to see who appeared to be familiar with whom, or if any crew members had tension between them.

Anything could prove to be useful.

Since Minho had primarily dealt with Lydecker up until that point, Fallon hadn't had much direct interaction with him. She observed him, exuding professionalism and authority, saying the right things at the right times, and behaving in all the ways a captain should.

So far, she'd found nothing to criticize him for, but she'd hardly expected this to be easy.

Fallon and Minho had both worked way more than double time since the crew's arrival. Captain Lydecker and his crew had immediately sprung into pre-coordinated shift schedules. Even the reception breakfast had been neatly organized around those schedules.

She wasn't sorry to see a legitimate mess hall spring to life, fully stocked and staffed. Rather than doctored packets and limited supplies, Asimov now had a full stock of fresh ingredients, and a regular delivery schedule to make sure it stayed that way.

Everything was falling into line.

That evening, Minho dropped by her quarters—her new, smaller quarters. She was no longer a ranking officer on the station, as a mere lieutenant, and had been assigned more modest accommodations accordingly.

"Hey," he said after entering, his eyes roaming the surroundings.

She didn't mind the smaller quarters. She still had plenty of room and comfort. More than she needed. Minho's quarters were further away though, now. Her next-door neighbor was now a pale-skinned Sarkavian who always regarded Fallon with poorly-veiled suspicion.

Why that was, Fallon didn't know. Mostly likely, it was simply that Fallon had been on the station when they arrived, but wasn't a member of the actual crew. That made her a bit of an outsider, and a possible rival, though it seemed ridiculous to her that anyone might look at it that way.

"Hey," she returned. "How's it going with the captain?"

He shrugged and sank onto her newly-assigned couch. It was smaller and less plush than her previous one, but it was good enough for her.

"By the book," he said.

"You sound tired."

"A little," he admitted. "There's been a lot going on. But good news—we're both getting the day off tomorrow. The day after, we'll start security drills."

"That's good," she said. "You'll get a chance to rest up. And three of the skeleton crew are leaving tomorrow on a transport. We'll get to say a proper goodbye."

"Should we?" he asked.

"Shouldn't we?" she countered. Regardless of the fact that he and she were there under false pretenses, the preparation crew had worked hard together to get the work done. It seemed right to say goodbye personally.

"We should," he said. "I just wanted to see if you'd change your mind if I challenged you."

"Never," she promised. "Can I get you something to drink?"

"Do you have any tea?" he asked.

"Am I Japanese?" she retorted, moving toward her small kitchenette without waiting for a reply.

"How would I know?" he asked. "Maybe it's just your cover identity."

"You got me." She put two mugs of water into the heat-ex. "I'm secretly a Briveen spy, here to make sure the PAC stays out of Briveen business."

"Wow," he said. "You're good. I can't even tell that your arms are cybernetic."

"That was nothing." She retrieved the tea packets. "Hiding my scales is the real killer."

When the tea was ready, she took it over and joined him on the couch. "So what are we doing tomorrow?"

"What do you mean?" He cautiously sipped his tea.

"I assume we won't be sleeping in and hitting the mess hall for fancy omelettes."

"Do they have those?" he asked, eyes wide. "Dang, I'm missing out. Why didn't you tell me?"

"Well, I've barely seen you the last couple days. That could have something to do with it."

"Well, get ready to be sick of me. We'll be in lockstep for the rest of this assignment."

She scrunched up her face into a terrible expression but said nothing.

He ignored her. "You're right. We won't be resting and relaxing tomorrow. I've already begun researching Lydecker's crew, and we need to organize some specialized surveillance."

Her heart sped up a little. "I am definitely on board with that. Everything's already in place. I just need to know where we want to pay particular attention. Then I can flag the security footage for specific scenarios that we want to view."

"We'll have to figure that out. At the moment, I have no particular suspects, outside of the captain himself. That means that for now, everyone's suspect."

"Right. And we have surveillance on the captain's correspondence?"

He nodded. "Yes. We'll need to review that carefully every day, as well. And that of any other key figures, should we identify any. Officially, as security experts, we're here to run two months' worth of drills, tests, and maintenance. Hopefully, we'll be able to find what we need to either prove or disprove the smuggling theory in that time."

"If not, then command will have to come up with a reason for us to stay longer."

"Exactly." He sipped his tea. "And if that's necessary, then it's what we'll have to do, but it's not ideal. It would be abnormal in this situation, since the new crew should be ready to take over all functions by then."

She held her teacup up. "To success in two months, then," she said.

He gently touched his cup to the side of hers in a toast. "To success," he agreed. "One way or another."

FALLON KEPT WATCHING CAPTAIN LYDECKER, trying to glean something about his personality that might suggest untrustworthiness. A willingness to overlook protocols that were superfluous to the situation, maybe, or a propensity to be too much of a stickler to compensate for secret dealings.

She saw none of that, though, only a middle-aged captain with an above-average understanding of advanced physics and a fondness for casserole-style dishes. The mess hall served those types of meals far too frequently for it to be a coincidence.

She sat in a conference room, watching him interact with his senior staff and department heads, ensuring that all portions of the crew were being administered to, managed, and guided into a routine of expected daily operations.

"Commander Stoyers, I've noticed that two junior officers who report to you have been late reporting to duty on two different occasions." Frowning, the captain looked up from the infoboard he held.

Stoyers nodded. "I believe they're in a relationship, sir. I've warned them that any further infractions will result in disciplinary action."

The captain held his gaze. "I consider personal relationships between crew members to be none of my business, unless it affects their work. I'm glad you gave them a warning, to allow them some leeway to ease into the new routine here, but we've been here two weeks and that's more than enough time. Anyone showing up late to their duty shifts or otherwise not performing as expected will not be indulged."

Those gathered either nodded or murmured their understanding.

"Good, then." The captain nodded. He turned his attention to Fallon. "Well, then, Lieutenant Arashi, I think it's fair to say that we are more than ready to begin security drills. Are you ready?"

All captains had their own personality and command style. Lydecker's tended to be a bit more formal and serious than most, but as he looked at her, she saw an almost imperceptible shift in his features. His eyes softened and while his mouth didn't turn up into a smile, the set of it relaxed.

For some reason, he liked her. Maybe it was because she'd made a couple of subtle, wry jokes when consulting with him and the security staff. Whatever it was, she hoped it proved to be something she could use to her advantage.

"Yes sir, all ready to go. I've drawn up a schedule and I'm just waiting for your order."

"Proceed," he said. "Is there any chance I won't be forced out of bed at some point?"

His lips turned up slightly in a small smile.

"None at all, sir," she assured him. "All crew will be thoroughly disrupted at the most inconvenient of times for fire drills, containment breach drills, evacuation drills, and all the rest. There will be no pattern to the drills, or hint that one is impending."

"I think it's fair to say," Minho said, "that a great deal of chaos can be expected, particularly the first couple of times we do each type of drill."

The captain nodded. "I suspect so. It should be a very eventful couple of weeks."

"I'm sure of it," Fallon said. "But once that's done, you'll be able to look forward to having the pleasure of kicking me off the station."

She gave him a small, knowing smile. After the crew had gotten the emergency drills down, all that would remain for her and Minho to do would be training the crew to pilot the drones. A few already had some experience.

His expression warmed again. "It's always good to have the end goal in sight, isn't it?"

Fallon smiled. Although he'd said it in an understated way, that was definitely a joke. She could almost start to like the man, if she didn't know he was a potential suspect. But then, maybe he wasn't guilty after all and she'd have a chance to like him for real.

Only time would tell.

"Is there anything else?" The captain looked around the table at the fourteen people gathered around him.

When no one else offered any new business, the captain pushed back his chair and stood. "All right then. You're all dismissed. Work hard today. We'll be getting a visit from the admiralty in a month so they can tour and inspect the station. I want us to be ready in half that time."

Fallon hid her smile at the crew's quiet body language. They knew they had a lot of things to do, learn, and perfect in a short amount of time. Since she wasn't part of that, outside of her own specific tasks, she had the luxury of being amused at their discomfort.

She was glad she didn't share those problems, though. She had plenty of her own unique issues to work through.

Like figuring out whether or not their captain was a criminal.

"Do you want to do it?" Fallon asked.

Minho smiled. "And take this away from you? I wouldn't dream of it."

"All right, then," she said. "Here we go."

From her quarters, she launched a program—its parameters already set—in the security office. She'd largely avoided the department because, as someone who wasn't a part of the regular crew complement, she didn't truly belong there while the security officers adjusted to their new posts, and also because she didn't want to give anyone any hints that a drill might be coming.

Immediately, alarms started going off. Emergency lighting flared, and alert lights glowed red.

All over the ship, systems would be locking down, preventing access and shunting power to critical systems.

"Oh, no," Minho said calmly. "It looks like the station's about to blow up."

"Yep," she agreed. "Let's see how that goes."

They strolled to the doors of her quarters, but once in the corridor, they both adjusted their body language so that it was appropriate to an emergency situation.

As they went, doors swished open and crew members came hurrying out, rushing this way or that way, depending on what their assigned emergency duties and escape routes were.

"Nobody's freaking out and screaming 'we're going to die!' yet," Minho noted pleasantly in a low tone. "So that's good."

"Most of them will be certain it's just a drill," she said. "But it would be good if they weren't sure."

"Working in a heightened emotional state would definitely be better practice for a real disaster," he agreed. "But they'll spring surprises on them down the line, after we're gone."

More people rushed by and Fallon felt satisfied that they seemed to be in a genuine hurry. Occasionally, she caught the sound of loud voices. Overall, she got the impression of uncertainty and urgency, which was reasonable for the situation.

She exchanged a veiled look with Minho. The evacuation of the station was proceeding as it should, although probably too slowly. That was expected, though, and the timing would improve drastically each time they ran through it.

For now, though, while everyone else was occupied and distracted, she and Minho had a different job to do. One that had a lot to do with security but nothing to do with evacuation.

By unspoken agreement, they proceeded to their first stop.

Asimov Station's second in command kept her quarters tidy. Fallon only got a glimpse as Minho entered. She remained in the corridor with her voicecom in her hand. If anyone came that way, she'd pretend to be giving orders to someone and hurry them along.

Inside, Minho would be following up on something they'd started before the crew had even arrived. Within each local voicecom display and panel inside the senior crew members' quarters, she and Minho had placed monitoring programs. Everything those officers did on the voicecom while inside their quarters would be recorded, as well as each time the officer left and returned to their quarters.

They'd been unwilling to risk transmission of that information, given that Lydecker had control of the station. Instead, they'd have to copy and purge the data, which was stored only locally, in person.

While everyone else was occupied with the drills, this was the perfect time.

In less than a minute, Minho returned, nodded to her, and they continued onward. If anyone happened to appear and see him entering or exiting, they would claim to be doing a sweep to make sure no souls remained on board.

This would be the longest drill they did, and the only time they did a full evacuation. Because it was critical to test all evacuation pods, everyone but Fallon and Minho would actually depart from the station. Even the captain. In future drills of this type, they would stop short of ejecting the pods and simply track the timing of all souls properly following protocol.

As they hurried on to the next officer's quarters, Fallon wondered what the remaining skeleton crew thought of having to participate in these drills when they were scheduled to depart very soon.

Again and again, Minho slipped into abandoned quarters, retrieved data storage, and escaped. When they arrived at Captain Lydecker's quarters, she palmed her comport and assumed the position, only to have Minho give a small shake of his head.

"Nope," he said. "You're going in on this one. Time to earn your stripes."

She blinked at him. They hadn't discussed this. His skills and experience qualified him as the one to do the data retrieval. Especially since they were about to get the information for their actual suspect.

She gathered herself and nodded. If he said she should do it, then she'd do it. She had few doubts about herself, but about him, she had none at all. If he said this was what they should do, then she would do it.

Quickly, she moved inside. The quarters were a mirror of those she'd occupied before the captain's arrival, and she went directly to the voicecom panel built into the wall. All other voicecom devices within the quarters had fed their data into this unit, so she only needed to extract the data from this one place.

"Captain?" she called out, wanting to ascertain that he had, in fact, left the quarters. After a moment of indecision, she checked the bedroom and the necessary.

Of course, no one was there. It would be unthinkable that the captain, or anyone else, would lounge around in the captain's quarters while an evacuation order was in place.

She returned to the voicecom, inserted a portable device, and used her thumbprint to activate the monitoring program. It only took seconds to take the already compacted data and upload it to the device. Once the device was ejected from the panel, all the data would be wiped from this location.

It was some very slick programming. She'd never seen anything like it when Minho had shown it to her.

Just as she had when she'd first seen the programming, she wondered what Raptor would think of it. Had he seen it already? What else had he seen?

Seconds could take a very long time, under the right circumstances. She stole a look at the doors to the quarters, willing them to remain shut.

There. Transfer complete.

She ejected the device, ensuring that no trace of its use or her presence in the quarters remained, and quickly exited.

Nodding to Minho, they proceeded to their next destination: the evacuation pods.

Only they could recall the pods for this exercise.

On the way, Minho made a shipwide announcement. "This is Lieutenant Commander Minho Park. Asimov Station is under an evacuation order. If any souls remain on board, respond directly to me now, so you can receive assistance."

They stood in a long corridor. It resembled a corridor with docking bays, but pods were much smaller and didn't have airlocks. Two hundred doors represented the entirety of the escaped crew.

No response came over the voicecom.

Minho activated his comport again. "Activate a scan for life, excepting this location."

Such scans weren't foolproof, but there was no reason to think anyone had chosen to remain behind. No one wanted to be the person who turned an evacuation drill into a failure. That kind of thing could severely damage, if not ruin, a career.

Fallon looked at Minho, and he returned her gaze. They waited, letting minutes pass.

Minho's comport made two sharp blip sounds. He glanced at it, then back at her. "Looks like we're alone."

It was an interesting feeling. The two of them, the only people on an entire space station.

"It's kind of romantic, isn't it?" Minho asked.

"Yeah, this is a unique feeling. Like being in a live ghost town. But that doesn't make sense, does it?" It had made sense in her head, but spoken aloud, it only sounded like an oxymoron.

"No, I get what you mean." He paused. "By the way, have I ever told you how beautiful you are?"

She rolled her eyes. "Are you ever serious?"

"In this kind of situation? Deadly serious. And yet…there's a certain dark humor that comes with it." The corners of his eyes crinkled.

"Yeah, I'm familiar with it." She thought back to her missions with her team. They'd cracked plenty of odd and inappropriate jokes, too. It must be a universal thing for this kind of work.

They waited another few long moments, then Minho nodded. "All right. I think we can consider this evacuation complete."

He activated his comport and entered a series of commands to end the evacuation simulation.

The alarm stopped and the lights returned to normal. Fallon breathed a sigh of relief. She'd tuned those things out as much as possible, but now that they were gone, their absence felt downright heavenly.

Minho took a breath. When he spoke again, his voice was deeper. More official. "Attention all hands of Asimov Station. The station has been cleared of threats. You are hereby authorized to return. This message will be certified with the pre-existing authority codes of Asimov Station."

He entered his authorization, then returned his comport to its place on his belt. "Well, that's that. One drill down, only about a billion to go."

"Not quite a billion," she said. "More like...fifty."

The new crew would learn to jump at a moment's notice in the next two weeks.

"Close enough," he said. "Also, don't forget that I made a pass at you and you rebuffed me. I'm offended. I demand you make amends."

She laughed at him. "Fine. I'll steal some food from the mess hall and make you dinner one night."

"Deal," he said. "But don't steal it. Appropriate it through proper channels. And see if there's anything in hydroponics you could use."

7

After the excitement of the evacuation drill, Fallon and Minho kept the crew on their toes with a variety of other drills.

In the meantime, the pair also experienced the polar opposite of emergency excitement.

Reviewing stolen data was, as it turned out, deadly dull. She and Minho had spent days slogging through mundane voicecom activity, from every request for a map of the station to every personal communication.

They viewed, categorized, then moved on to the next thing. Thus far, nothing had seemed suspicious, but it was possible that patterns might emerge, so they wouldn't know anything for sure until they'd gotten through all the data and looked for outliers and commonalities.

They'd gone through Captain Lydecker's data first. When nothing seemed out of place, Fallon said, "Maybe he's clean."

"Maybe he's careful," Minho countered.

"Maybe's he's waiting," she suggested.

He'd joined her in her quarters for the meal she'd promised him. She'd managed to get good ingredients to make him some gimbap and samgyeopsal. She hoped the traditional dishes from

Korea made him happy. The meat was easy enough to make, but the seaweed in the gimbap proved challenging. She shredded it twice before looking for a better way to roll the sea vegetable around the rice.

"Wow," he said after he dug into the meal. "This isn't terrible. At all."

She put on an offended look. "Hey, I'm perfectly capable of looking up someone else's work and copying it. I absolutely don't hate this."

She used her chopsticks to pop a bite of pork into her mouth.

He grinned. "It's good. Thanks. It doesn't exactly remind me of my grandmother's cooking, but it's a solid effort at Korean cooking."

"I was going for 'delicious' but I guess that faint praise will have to do." In truth, she was pleased with the faint praise. She'd been concerned that she had massacred one of his childhood favorites or something.

"Like I said, it's good." He shoved a slice of gimbap into his mouth and chewed with exaggerated vigor to prove it. "Most of all because you took the time to do something very considerate that you thought might please me. And it did."

"Did? Past tense? You're over it?"

He laughed. "You're relentless. Did, and still does. See?" He shoved several pieces of samgyeopsal into his mouth at once and chewed. It was far too much food for one mouthful, and he looked ridiculous.

She smiled. "You're cute when you act stupid. But you're welcome. I'm glad you like it."

"What were your favorite Japanese favorites, growing up?" he asked. "Maybe something special your mom or dad made, or a grandmother or something."

It was the closest he'd ever come to asking details about her family or specifics about her past.

"Tonkatsu. It's pork, but not barbequed like this. It's breaded and fried. I'm sure you've had it."

He nodded and she continued, "Udon and sushi were always around for birthdays and other celebrations, or just for an everyday thing. But when I think about what made me happiest when I was a kid, I have to say it was ramen. Homemade, not from a packet. My mom always teased me because I wanted an egg stirred into the sauce and a soft-boiled egg on top, too. She called me 'Chicken' sometimes because of it."

She paused, thinking back to how she felt when she ate the ramen her mother made her. "Ramen, for me, was like a ritual. Putting my face in the bowl and taking a deep inhale of the aroma while feeling the steam on my skin. Carefully slurping the broth while it was still too hot, so it didn't burn my tongue. Eating the boiled egg first, and then finally, digging into the noodles. To me, that's the taste and the feel of my childhood home."

She looked up and realized he'd stopped eating. He was just watching her, smiling.

"What?" she asked defensively.

"Nothing." He shoved a piece of gimbap into his mouth.

"Well, what about you, then?" she asked. She felt a little exposed after telling him something so real about her past. "What reminds you of your childhood?"

He looked toward the ceiling of her quarters with a thoughtful expression, still chewing. "Gimbap was always around. For what you're describing, though, I think I'd have to say tteokbokki. I could never resist it. And you'll probably think it's weird, but Bennite stew. My dad was really good at making it."

He looked so nostalgic, with a sweet smile on his lips. He must have some really fond memories wrapped around those dishes.

"You're cute when you're sentimental," she said.

He snapped out of his reverie and blinked at her. "What?"

She'd been waiting to say something like that to him after his joke about her being beautiful during the first evacuation drill. It was a bonus that he really did look quite endearing.

"Eat your rice," she told him.

After a quick grin, he ate every bite.

FALLON MADE sure to say a personal goodbye to each of the members of the skeleton crew when they left Asimov. Other than Katheryn Lee and Priestley Simkopf, who were continuing on as part of the station's crew, only Jess and Jacen remained. Fallon checked in on them regularly, and kept tabs on them. There was no reason she should, really, except that she felt a sense of personal duty toward them.

Jess had intended to leave much sooner, but her transport had fallen through and she couldn't book another for a full month. As a result, she had to cancel her plans for a vacation and go from Asimov straight to her next job.

She was surly about it, too. She could often be heard muttering, "Bloody Rescan transports."

Fortunately, there were no Rescans on board at that time.

At the moment, Fallon's life consisted of emergency simulations, surveillance, and suspicion. She and Minho had done two more data grabs during drills, and while there was no single thing that looked suspicious, a couple of patterns had emerged.

Captain Lydecker followed almost exactly the same routine every day. He woke and went to bed at the same time, took meals at the same times, and worked through his duties in the same order. On days that were disrupted by drills, he adjusted his schedule in a way to accomplish the same tasks with as much similarity to his regular routine as possible.

Except for every fourth day. For some reason, on every fourth day, he got up earlier, stayed up later, and skipped breakfast.

Thus far, Fallon and Minho couldn't figure out why.

The other pattern they identified involved the crew. Lydecker's first officer, and the person who was second in command of the station, had exhibited some off behavior. Commander Torra Eidel had seemed to be highly organized, based on the condition in which she kept her quarters. But for some reason, she frequently showed up three to eight minutes late for her duty shifts. The login and logout times of her work shifts clearly showed behavior that should have prompted action on the captain's part.

But the records showed that Lydecker had taken no action. At least, if he had, it hadn't been an official action, as he'd written nothing at all about these incidents.

Minho and Fallon had been unable to find any evidence of him disciplining her in person, either.

A very unusual scenario.

When she went to Minho's quarters to review the previous day's activity on the station, she expressed her concerns.

"Are we going to have enough time to complete a thorough investigation?"

"What do you mean?" Minho asked.

"So far, we've found nothing incriminating. Just a couple of oddities. We might not have enough time to find the reason for those oddities."

He flipped through screens showing the activity reports for the previous day's night shift. "If we don't find anything incriminating, then that's the result we have. Our goal is not to find proof of guilt. It's to investigate. A lack of results is still results. If PAC command wanted us to remain until we could find something to nail Lydecker for, they would have given us a different cover."

"Why not give us a cover that ensures we can exhaust all the possibilities, though?" she asked.

He shifted his attention to her. "If command wanted us to know that, they'd have told us. We perform the job they give us, under the parameters they choose. Everything else is part of their larger game plan, which we don't get to know."

She chewed on that idea for a full minute before asking, "Do you think it's likely that we're here under a pretense, and that the job we're actually doing is not the one we think we're doing?"

He smiled. "You're catching on."

"Do you think that's what this is?" she pressed.

"I don't think it is, and I don't think it isn't. Or to be more precise, I don't think about anything that isn't the specific mission I was told to accomplish. Focus on what's ahead of you. If you ever make it to senior command, then it will become your job to play multilevel galactic chess. Until then, you're just one of the game pieces."

She frowned. That didn't fit at all with her proactive, fight-hard philosophy.

He patted her on the shoulder. "It's not as bad as it sounds. Think of it this way—you get to fly in, kick ass, and ditch out instead of sitting in an office, plotting and making decisions."

"That does sound better," she admitted.

"Perspective is everything."

They finished going through the data for the previous shift.

"I'm not seeing anything here," Minho said. "I've set up lunch with Katheryn today. It'll just look like a casual meal, but I want to talk to her about Priestley."

"Priestley? Why?"

"I've heard some whispers that the captain doesn't like him. I want to get Katheryn's take on it."

"Is Priestley being treated poorly?" She didn't like the idea of the guy being unfairly targeted. Just because he wasn't as social as other people wasn't a reason to treat him poorly. He always did his job well.

"There's nothing on the record, but I want to see if anything's going on off the record. I dislike the idea of leaving him here if it's going to be a bad situation for him."

She liked that he, like her, seemed to feel a sense of responsibility to those who had previously been under his command. "What could we do, if that were the case?"

"I don't know. Put in a word at command that he should be transferred, maybe. More likely, just smoothing things over a little would do the trick. You know, find out if there's been some misunderstanding and sort it out."

"Okay. It'll be nice to see Katheryn. I'm curious about her take on the captain. And whether she's heard anything about how her fellow command officers feel about him."

Minho nodded. "Me too."

She clapped her hands together. "Okay, I think it's drill time. What should we do today?"

He thoughtfully pursed his lips. "How about collision emergency, scenario two?"

"We did that one two days ago."

"Exactly. They'll expect a different scenario and be looking for a different solution."

She smiled. "I like it. Collision scenario two it is."

He paused and eyed her. "Admit it. You like making a whole space station dance to your tune."

"It does have a certain charm," she said. "Maybe I'm destined to sit in the big command chair at Jamestown, after all."

He pretended to shudder and put a hand over his heart. "May Prelin protect us."

When Fallon arrived at Minho's quarters for lunch, Katheryn already sat at the table, sipping tea.

"Am I late?" Fallon checked the chronometer on her comport.

Katheryn bowed at the waist from her sitting position. Since they were in a casual setting and had agreed to be informal in the past, it wasn't necessary to bow, but she probably did it out of habit.

"No, I was early," Katheryn said. "I always plan extra time to get anywhere, because I expect to get stopped and asked about this or that."

Minho walked over from the kitchenette and placed a cup in front of Fallon, then poured tea into it. "Ah, I bet as the lowest-ranking member of the command crew, you get all the questions that people can't or don't want to ask of the senior staff."

"You're right about that. I've gotten everything from, 'Does the captain ever relax?' to, 'Is the security liaison single?'" She laughed.

"Well, Minho is kind of cute, in his own way," Fallon said, chuckling with her.

"They weren't talking about him," Katheryn said.

"Oh." Fallon had assumed that any personal interest would be directed toward him.

Minho found it quite amusing, judging by his grin.

"For the record," Fallon said, "I'm not in a relationship, but I'm not available either. I have too much going on in my career to deal with dating right now."

"I'll just tell them you're involved," Katheryn decided. "That's more likely to discourage them."

It was also the truth, though Katheryn thought it wasn't, which was a bit ironic.

Minho joined them at the table with his own cup of tea. "The food will be ready in a few minutes. It just needs to sit and cool a little. So what do you think of Lydecker, for real, off the record?"

"Hmm." Katheryn looked down into her tea. "He's methodical. Professional. A very by-the-book kind of guy. He's a little... formal. But maybe that will relax a little once he feels like he's established order here and ensured that the station runs well. Maybe after the admirals tour the station?" She shrugged. "Or maybe he doesn't loosen up with crew at all. Either way, it seems like he'll be okay to work for."

"Have you heard of any issues between him and the crew?" Minho asked.

Though his tone was entirely casual, as if he'd just thought of the question, Katheryn straightened. "Why, have you heard something?"

Answering a question with a question indicated that maybe she had heard of something noteworthy.

Fallon wondered if Katheryn might be savvy enough to have used this get-together to do her own reconnaissance on the captain.

If so, that would certainly be interesting, and add a new facet to Fallon's understanding of the woman.

Fallon looked to Minho.

"We've noticed a couple of odd things. But we don't want to go poking around where we shouldn't. Is there anything we should know?"

She pressed her lips together, as if preventing words from leaving of their own volition. Then she said, "He and the first officer seem very familiar. More than I'd have expected. And she arrives late on a regular basis, with no explanation. Nobody has said anything, but I can tell everyone's wondering about it."

Minho and Fallon exchanged a look.

"What do you think it is?" Katheryn asked, glancing from one to the other.

"We noticed something odd there, too," Fallon admitted. "But it could be any number of things that are entirely official or on the level. How a captain handles his crew is up to him. But it is odd, isn't it?"

"Yeah," Katheryn said. "It's gone on too long and is too obvious for it not to be strange."

"We'll do a little careful looking," Minho said. "Also, I think it's possible he has an issue with Priestley," he said. "I wanted to see what I could find out about that."

A crease appeared between Katheryn's eyebrows. "I hadn't heard that. But I haven't followed up with him and the other contractors much." She ducked her head. "I should have thought to do that."

Minho said gently, "You're new to being a command officer. You've been swamped."

"Still. I should have looked out for him and the others better. I'll look into it."

"Carefully," Minho warned. "We don't want anyone talking about it or taking notice. There's no reason for you to get on the captain's bad side."

"That would make for an awful three or four years, wouldn't it?" She grimaced.

"I've heard some horror stories of people who clashed with their commanding officers," he said. "Let's avoid that, for sure."

He got up and started bringing the food over. He set large bowls in front of Katheryn, then Fallon, then sat down with one for himself.

Fallon stared in surprise at the food he'd made.

"What is this?" Katheryn asked.

"Ramen," Minho said. "Traditional Japanese dish. Emiko mentioned it the other day and it's been on my mind, so I thought I'd take a whack at it."

In each bowl, two neat halves of a soft-boiled egg carefully nestled on top of the noodles, which were surrounded by a light-brown broth. She'd bet a thousand credits there was an egg cooked into the broth, too.

She smiled at him, touched.

He smiled back. "The noodles should be at the perfect texture right now. We should eat before they get soggy."

They dug in. While they didn't taste exactly like the ones she'd eaten growing up, they were delicious.

As they ate, and for a while afterward, they chatted about the crew, the drills, and general life on the station.

"Another restaurant opened today," Katheryn said. "And two more stores open tomorrow. The remaining medical crew will arrive by the end of the week. We're almost all together."

"It's a shame we won't be here to see it when it's one hundred percent complete," Fallon said.

"You'll have to come visit when you have a chance," Katheryn said.

It didn't seem likely, since Fallon and Minho were using false identities. But who knew? It was always possible they could be sent back under those same identities, or be disguised as someone else. Surely at some point, in one method or another, she'd return to Asimov.

"I'd love to," Fallon said. "Though this is a bit out of the way. It would be a little tough to just drop by on my way somewhere else."

"Yes," Katheryn agreed. "But I hope I'll see you sometime, all the same."

The lieutenant arched her back and stretched. "Well, I should get to sleep. You never know when someone will set off alarms in the middle of the night."

Fallon and Minho chuckled.

"It was good catching up with you," Fallon said.

"Let me know if you hear anything about any friction between the captain and any of the people here," Minho added. "I'd like to help smooth things over, if I can."

"I will. And thanks again for the food." Katheryn waved before walking out the doors.

After they closed again and Fallon and Minho were alone, she asked, "What are the odds of us being sent back here at some point?"

"As good as anything, I guess." He stacked the dishes and took them into the kitchenette. "But we're usually involved in things that are against the odds, so taking that into consideration, I don't know if that makes it more or less likely."

"Well, that was confusing."

He turned to face her and smiled. "I'm tired. Someone keeps setting off alarms when I'm sleeping."

She walked into the kitchenette to get a cloth so she could wipe the table off. "Yeah, that was you."

"And you," he pointed out, moving to the sink and turning the water on to start washing the bowls.

"But mostly you." She retrieved a towel, then reached around him to wet it under the faucet.

"There's no 'mostly' with running a drill. There either is a drill, or there is not a drill."

She went to the table and started wiping it off with long, smooth strokes. "You're being pedantic."

"I am not," he argued. "I'm being factual."

She returned to the kitchenette and wiped the counter, then turned around and leaned back against it. "Thank you for making ramen, by the way. It was very sweet of you."

He set the last bowl aside to dry, turned off the water, and looked at her. "You're welcome."

"I wasn't happy about having my team split up," she said, all traces of humor and teasing gone. "But I'm glad that you were on this mission with me."

"Want to know something?" he asked.

"What?" she asked.

"When I received the assignment to go to the academy and work with you, I didn't want to. Really didn't want to. I asked for a different assignment, and I've never done that. But then I met you, and you were green and disliked me immediately, but I liked you right away."

"I didn't dislike you," she said. "I just didn't know you, and I definitely didn't trust you."

"Ah." His voice was soft.

She became aware of the fact that he was just centimeters away. That wasn't unusual, since they often sparred or worked together in small spaces. But the mood had changed. There was an atmosphere of…something.

Chemistry. There was a strong pull between them. She felt it, and knew from the unguarded look on his face that he did, too.

Was it her imagination, or had he just shifted closer?

"Emergency alert!" she blurted.

He blinked and took a step back. "What?"

"Let's do a life support failure drill." Realizing she was still holding the wet cloth, she dropped it in the sink and marched to the voicecom.

"Aw, no, not a life support drill. I hate rebreathers. They chap my lips and make my throat sore."

"Yep. Life support." She entered the commands and activated the program for life support emergency scenario one.

Immediately, the voicecom systems came alive.

"They're really going to hate us tomorrow," he warned. "Two drills in one day."

"Good thing we'll only be here a few weeks, then, right? Let's go." She led the way, marching out confidently.

Inside, though, she wondered if she'd just avoided a crisis of a different kind.

8

THE FOLLOWING DAY, Fallon went to visit Jess, Jacen, and Priestley. Jacen was scheduled to leave the next day, so she wanted a chance to talk to him, but more importantly she wanted to follow up on the question of whether Captain Lydecker had been treating him unfairly.

She didn't intend to run any emergency procedures after having done two the previous day. First, because people needed a chance to do their actual work, as there was a lot of it. Second, because the crew would probably be expecting one, which made the exercise less valuable.

She went to see her three former subordinates individually, so they could speak in private. She dropped by Jess's quarters first.

"Welcome to my shoebox," Jess said, stepping back so Fallon could enter.

She was joking, but not by much. As someone who was neither currently employed at the station nor someone renting space as a transient, she'd been relegated to a tiny sleeping room with no kitchenette and only a basic necessary with a portable sonic shower.

"Have a seat." Jess pointed. "You can choose between the middle of the bed and the foot of the bed."

She wasn't joking.

Fallon sat at the foot of the bed. "At least it's clean and quiet. And no bad smells."

"Oh, you've been to the loud, dirty, and stinky place too, huh? Yeah, I hate it there."

"You're a lot more cheerful than I thought you'd be, after getting stranded here," Fallon observed.

"What am I going to do? Spend a few weeks banging my head on the bulkhead? At least this place is easy living, and they're comping me my room and unlimited access to the mess hall."

"That's a relief."

Jess snorted. "The PAC is lucky they decided to do that. If they'd charged me to be stranded out here in the middle of nowhere, this place would have come down with a bad case of the gremlins."

"What do you mean?"

Jess leaned against the bulkhead. "Old mechanic trick. If the employer caused problems, they'd find themselves facing a lot of inexplicable failures and false alarms. There used to be ghost stories about little critters that could infest places and cause such problems. But it was just the engineers and mechanics."

Fallon laughed.

"Never piss off the people who take care of your hardware."

"It's a good rule to live by," Fallon said.

"So what brings you by?" Jess asked. "Missing the old days before all these people arrived?"

"Just thought I'd see how you were doing, since we haven't been crossing paths. Why, do you dislike the station's crew?"

She shrugged. "They're like any other. Mostly fine, with some notable exceptions. That's just people anywhere."

"Which notable exceptions?" Fallon asked.

Jess's gaze sharpened. "What are you digging for?"

"Nothing really," Fallon said casually. "I just figured if anyone had the gossip from around here, it would be you. The real stuff, though, not the silly junk about who might be hooking up with who."

"Hm, true, I do have a way of knowing things. But not here, really. Not since all the officers arrived."

"What about those of you from the skeleton crew?" Fallon asked. "Have any of them had any issues?"

Jess pressed her lips together, a thoughtful expression on her face. "Katheryn's experiencing a little hazing. Nothing to worry about, just some minor pranks from the mid-level command officers as they test her mettle."

"She didn't mention that," Fallon said. "You're sure it's nothing to be concerned about? She's just paying her dues?"

"Yeah. Just messing with her a bit. Telling her the captain's in the corridor and wants to see her when he's not, that kind of thing."

"Okay," Fallon said. "What else?"

Jess hesitated.

"What?" Fallon pressed.

"This might be the gossip type of thing, but it might be relevant, too." She shrugged. "Whatever. The first officer is pregnant."

"Commander Eidul's expecting a baby?" Fallon blinked in surprise. She'd been prepared for Jess to say a lot of things, but that news took her entirely by surprise.

"Yep. Experiencing a lot of health issues, too, but since the father doesn't know, she doesn't want the crew to know yet either. She wants to tell him in person, apparently. I imagine there have been whispers about her."

"Yes," Fallon admitted. "Though I don't think a pregnancy was a popular theory. It's good to know that it's a personal issue and not something else."

No wonder Captain Lydecker hadn't informed the rest of the

crew about the reason for Torra Eidel's odd job performance. He was being discreet.

"Like favoritism?" Jess asked.

"Exactly. How did you find out about the first officer?"

Jess smiled. "People at the lower rungs talk. I have a friend who's a medical tech. Don't ask me who, though. I won't tell."

"I wouldn't dream of it. Speaking of friends, have you heard anything from Priestley? I'm curious how he's doing with his new assignment."

"The job's fine," Jess said. "But on the three or four occasions he's crossed paths with the captain, the captain has had something negative to say to him. His uniform was too dirty, or he was making too much noise, or something like that. Things that would be no big deal if they were true, but they weren't."

"Hm." Fallon folded her hands in her lap. "Any idea why the captain would dislike him?"

"No. He's a quiet kid who gets his job done. He does tend to get nervous around authority figures, so maybe he just gets edgy when the captain's around, and the captain notices that he seems shifty."

"Maybe." Fallon hoped it was that simple. "And Jacen?"

"That kid would be popular on a deserted planet. He's got all the charm to get along on a place like this. He's been hanging out with a cute ensign, but you said you didn't want to hear about that kind of thing."

Fallon smiled. "Yeah, it's not really my business if it's unrelated to station operations in any way."

"Ah well," Jess gave her a playful smile. "It's just a fling anyway. Truth be told, I'm a little jealous. Wouldn't mind a bit of a fling myself, but of course, I'm too old for most of the people here."

"So what are you keeping busy with?" Fallon asked. "I hope you're not bored."

"Nah. I'm still taking the vacation I intended to have. I'm just doing it in a different way. I thought about taking a transport over to Bennaris, but I'd have to pay living expenses there. So I read. I watch holo-vids. I sleep as much as I want and as long as I like. Well," she amended, "outside of any bloody drills."

There was really no reason Jess should have to participate in drills, since she wasn't remaining on the station.

"Tell you what," Fallon said. "For the rest of the drills, how about you lock yourself in your quarters? I'll omit it from life sign reads, if there are any. I'll make it so your quarters and comport won't register the drills. So if the alarm lights flare in here, it's for real, and you'd better be sure to haul ass out of there."

"You'd do that?" Jess perked up. "Wow, that would be great. I'll just buy some earplugs for when I'm working, and I'll be set. Thanks."

"Good." Fallon checked the time. "I should get going. I wanted to talk to Jacen before Priestley gets off his shift, then see him immediately after. But if there's anything I can do for you, or anything you think I should know, be sure to contact me, okay? And let's get together for a meal in the next few days. We'll make the guys come with us, too."

"I like it. Thanks for stopping by, Emiko. It was really nice of you to bother with me."

Fallon paused at the doorway, surprised. "You're a valuable worker and person, Jess. People in uniforms aren't the only ones who are worth knowing."

She ducked out. Jacen's quarters were in the same section, so she went there next.

"No offense," Jacen said, "but I can't wait to leave here."

"Really?" Fallon asked. "I heard there was a certain ensign you were making the most of your time here with."

He laughed. "Yeah, well, you know. It's not like it's serious. But what is serious is my need for some sunshine and fresh air. I never realized how much I enjoy being planetbound."

Jacen was easy to talk to, and a half hour slipped by in no time. He tended to hang out with rookie officers, and didn't have any info he thought he should share with her.

"I'm nobody, so nobody tells me anything," he said with a chuckle.

He hadn't heard anything about Priestley, but fortunately he had met up with him regularly.

At least Priestley had one friend on board. For the time being, anyway.

"I'll come see you off tomorrow, just so you can feel good about someone waving as you leave," she promised before hurrying to catch Priestley coming off his work shift.

As a resident of the station, albeit on the lowest end of the contract workers, he had quarters in a crew section.

Unfortunately, he wasn't in his quarters. She'd checked the schedule, and he wasn't on duty. She'd wanted to drop in on him unexpectedly to avoid giving him the chance to put her off. She had a feeling he would, if he was experiencing difficulties. It was just a sense she had, but her understanding of him indicated that he would turn inward when he was having difficulties.

Since she didn't have time to search the station for him, she activated her comport. "Priestley, this is Emiko. I'm at your quarters. Do you have a few minutes? I need to talk to you. I can come to wherever you are."

A few moments later, he answered. "I'm in the gym. I can come meet you."

He sounded very slightly out of breath.

"I don't want to cut your exercise short. I'll come run with you. Unless you were almost done."

"No, just started. But I can do it later."

"And deprive me of a run?" she asked. "No way. I'll be there in ten minutes, so don't wear yourself out before I get there."

She immediately closed the channel to prevent him from arguing. Talking to him while doing some activity would probably be more comfortable for him than sitting face to face anyway.

Rather than drop by her quarters for her own workout gear, she'd change in the locker room and use some basic PAC standard issue that the station kept available for convenience.

She hurried to the gym. She didn't want to give Priestley time to psyche himself out and quit running.

As she went, she noticed a few looks of concern as people saw her. They probably thought she was on her way to initiate a drill.

She laughed quietly to herself. It was good that they were on alert. They needed to stay that way.

In record time, she arrived, changed, and charged up the stairs to join Priestley on the running track that ran the perimeter of the gym's walls, above the rest of the space.

"Hey," she said as she caught up to him.

"Hey," he echoed.

"How's it going under the new command? Lots of adjustments, right?"

"It's fine," he said.

She decided to cut right to the point. "I've heard you might be experiencing some difficulties with command. Lydecker in particular. Is that true?"

His pace suddenly slowed.

She sensed him internally arguing with himself. As a member of this crew, even as a contractor, his loyalty belonged with the captain. On the other hand, he knew her first, and had worked under her, too. Plus, they'd formed something of a rapport.

She jogged along, giving him time to decide what he wanted to say.

"I just have a lot to learn," he said. "I'm lacking. But I'll improve."

She hadn't ever found him lacking in anything except confidence and social skills. "What do you mean by lacking?"

His pace slowed again. Now they were barely going along at more than a fast walk.

"I've met the captain exactly twice. Both times, he took issue with me. It was embarrassing."

Though he said nothing more, she had a feeling that those interactions had been a lot more bothersome to him than he let on.

"I'm here to help, Priestley. I need to know the details."

He let out a sigh, slowing to a walk. "The first time I met him, I had just crawled out of the air containment system. As you probably know, it gets filthy in there. I was dirty. Lydecker took one look at me and said, 'Is this an Atalan refugee or a member of my crew?'"

His cheeks flamed red.

"I'm guessing he didn't say it in a joking tone," Fallon said. Even if he had, it was a cruel thing to say. There were several Atalans on board. The civil war on their planet had been going on for quite some time and showed no signs of ending anytime soon.

"No," Priestley answered.

"And the second time you met him?"

Priestley slowed to a stop and leaned back against the railing that looked out over the gym. "He was, as he usually is, flanked by his top three officers. I was helping unload a transport ship. The hover cart I was using had a power fluctuation and it tipped just enough to cause a box to fall. It made a loud noise and everyone looked at me."

"And?" Fallon prompted when he fell silent.

His shoulders came up, giving him the look of someone trying to shrink out of view. "Nobody said anything. The captain just...had this look. I felt like he was deciding right then that he was going to find a reason to get rid of me." He added quickly, "Dismiss me from the station, I mean."

It could be paranoia. Priestly could be misinterpreting the captain's expression and body language, since he didn't know Lydecker well. The man was quite stiff and foreboding.

But since others had noticed, and someone else had alerted Fallon to the situation first, she thought it more likely that Priestley's interpretation was correct.

"It's probably just me," he said. "I'm being too defensive, or I'm just not good enough to be here."

He didn't meet her gaze, looking down at his feet.

"I don't think so," she said.

He looked up at her.

She continued. "I've always found your judgment to be accurate. I trust it. There might be some reason for the friction, but I don't believe you're at fault. I'm going to look into it before I leave here, okay?"

His eyebrows rose in surprise. He seemed to be struggling to decide what to say. He settled on, "Why?"

She smiled gently. "Because I take care of my own. That means you, and this station as a whole. You're a good worker. You'll be an asset to Asimov. I owe it to you, the station, and Captain Lydecker to make sure you're able to do your job without stressing out or second-guessing yourself. That will only lead to problems. Plus, if you quit, they'd be losing a hard worker."

"I can't quit," he mumbled.

"Why's that?" she asked.

He met her gaze. "I have nowhere else to go. I don't have the money to live on my home planet. I don't have money to relocate to another planet. One way or another, I need to make this work."

She reached out and put her hand on his shoulder. "Then I'll help you make that happen."

He seemed at a loss for words again, and she let her arm fall and stepped back. To free him of the need to speak, she said, "I need to get back to work now, but keep me posted on what's going on with you, okay? You don't have to handle this alone."

He nodded and she turned away.

"Give me a daily report. If you don't, I'll come looking for you." She smiled to make sure the words didn't come across as threatening, but she meant it. "I won't be able to leave here with a clear conscience if you're struggling. So let's take care of this. I'll expect to hear from you this evening."

Before he could respond, she walked quickly away and descended the stairs to the lower level.

She would have preferred a good, hard run, but that wasn't consistent with her story of needing to get back to work. Instead, she removed the loaner shorts and shirt, dropped them into the processor to get cleaned and disinfected, and put her uniform on.

Back to work. She had a lot to do, and not much time to do it.

"ANYTHING?" Fallon leaned over Minho's shoulder to look at the voicecom. They'd done what they expected to be their final data grab during one of the last emergency scenarios.

The station's security staff were running the drills now, and none of it involved the two of them, except for evaluation purposes.

"Lydecker has remained true to his pattern of every fourth day being unusual. I'd hoped to figure out why, but there's nothing." Minho frowned at the screen.

"Are we still scheduled to meet with him this afternoon?"

He turned to look at her and she took a step back. "Why wouldn't we be?"

"I don't know. Just wondered if we'd gotten bumped to another time due to super important captain stuff."

"Nope. We're on target. How did you want to handle the meeting?"

"I was thinking we could give him an overall evaluation of the security team, the improvement in the emergency procedures drills, and kind of do an official handoff. Like we say we're available to assist with anything over the next few days, but we think everything's right on track. And then we can slide in the bit about Priestley somewhere."

"Ah. Sneaky-style, then."

"Sure, why not? We're the covert ops type, right?"

"Sure," he agreed. "I'm sure we can find a place to mention Priestley and press the captain a bit. I have to wonder if Lydecker might be experiencing some subconscious bias."

"Because Priestley isn't an officer?"

"Not just that," Minho said. "He's got one of the most menial, low-ranking jobs on the station, and he's a Zerellian from a very poor background. The captain is also Zerellian. I wonder if he has an issue with such a person representing his home planet."

"Possible," Fallon said. "A captain should be better than that, though. It's not like Priestley asked to grow up poor."

"Everyone has biases. Even captains. No matter how hard we try, our values and expectations are drilled into us, and sometimes it's the most subconscious stuff that comes out. Hopefully, once we subtly point it out, we can smooth things over for Priestley. Or, in the case that he has actually done something to offend the captain, we can deal with that. Either way, I'll feel better about leaving if we know he's situated."

"I thought the same thing," she admitted. "It's not his fault he doesn't have Jacen's ease. I know how it feels to have to make an effort. We can't all be naturally popular, like you."

He grinned. "Who said it came naturally? For all you know, I was a total outcast as a kid. People might have thrown garbage at me when they passed and called me gutter trash. I might have had some serious trauma, which might have been the impetus for my going to the academy and becoming an officer. Maybe that's even why I wanted to get into covert ops—so I could wreak havoc on people in general."

"Is that the case?" she asked.

"No. But you didn't know that."

She chuckled. "I really didn't think so."

She liked this. The weird moment of chemistry they'd had that one night hadn't repeated itself. They were just comfortable, fun, and in sync.

"Stick with me, little grasshopper," he said. "I'll teach you the ways of the galaxy."

"Ugh. That's the worse holo-vid paraphrased quote I've ever heard. I'm leaving now. Don't try to stop me. I'll see you later at the meeting with the captain."

"Don't pretend you didn't like it," he said as she stepped toward the door. "We both know you're secretly in awe of my super cool vid-quoting skills."

She shot him a raised eyebrow of extreme dubiousness before ducking out of his quarters.

"WE'VE BEEN PLEASED with how quickly the crew has gotten up to speed," Minho concluded. "We think they're ready to take over all operations, with no assistance or oversight. With your approval, of course, sir."

"That's good to hear," Captain Lydecker said. "Of course, I'll trust your judgment, and theirs, and approve your suggestion."

"Of course, we'll be available for consult until we leave, and will be evaluating for official purposes, but at this point it's just protocol." Minho smiled easily. "Asimov Station is in good hands."

Lydecker nodded. "I agree. We have a good crew here."

Minho used that opportunity to segue into the other matter.

"Is there anyone who isn't performing up to your expectations, sir? There's still time to make changes."

Lydecker frowned thoughtfully. "No startup is perfect, and there have been a few bobbles here and there. I think it will all shake out just fine. I see no need to replace anyone."

Fallon looked to Minho. Would he press further? She would have, given her feeling of responsibility for Priestley, but that might be a mistake.

She'd leave it to Minho to decide.

"What about Priestley Simkopf?" Minho asked. "I've heard some things."

Fallon hid a smile. He'd brought it up, and by being vague about what he'd heard, he could imply that others might have complained about the young Zerellian.

"Who?" the captain asked.

"A low-level maintenance and custodial worker," Minho answered. "I believe you've crossed paths with him a couple times, and might not have found him entirely satisfactory."

Lydecker frowned again, more deeply this time. "I think I might know who you mean. Young Zerellian man, looks a little...well, rough?"

Since Priestley wore the same work outfit as any of the other maintenance people, there seemed no reason to think of him as rough-looking. Was that an indication that the captain had a bias against him because of his background?

But the captain had denied any particular knowledge of Priestley. If that were true, he wouldn't know the young man's background.

Fallon kept her mouth shut, waiting to see how Minho played the conversation.

"A young Zerellian, yes," Minho conceded. "I've never noticed that he looks rough, but he does crawl around in the bowels of the station, so it's entirely possible you saw him at an inopportune moment." Minho smiled. "Some types of work are just dirtier than others, aren't they?"

Fallon had an odd sense that Minho was not only making a point of the nature of Priestley's work, but also making a point of the difference between contract workers and officers, and the expectations thereof.

After a pause, the captain said, "That's true. Like I said, I don't think anyone needs to be replaced at this point. I think everyone will settle into life on Asimov just fine."

Minho nodded. "Glad to hear it, sir. If that should change while I'm still here, I'd be happy to facilitate any replacement assignments. I want to be sure I leave here knowing I've done everything I can to ensure an ideal beginning."

"I appreciate your eye for detail," Lydecker said. "In your shoes, a lot of officers would be looking to slack off and enjoy a few days of rest before shipping out. Your dedication is noted."

There was a note of dismissal in the captain's voice.

"We're at your disposal, until the very end, Captain," Minho said.

Minho and Fallon bowed, then left the meeting room.

THE MISSION WAS WINDING DOWN. Minho joined Fallon to see Jacen off. They had no more official duties, other than monitoring the security team in a hands-off kind of way. They used their remaining time to scrutinize every move Captain Lydecker made.

Sometimes they used her quarters, but mostly they used his, since they were larger. She was pretty sure they would wear indentations into the couch before they left, due to how much time they spent hovering over the voicecom display.

"If he's up to anything, he's got some very underground way of communicating about it," Minho said. "And that seems unlikely, given how far out of the way we are from most PAC traffic. It looks like he's clean, at least now. Maybe in the past he wasn't, but that's for someone else to uncover."

"So what now?" Fallon asked. "Will I be returned to my team?"

He took a long moment to answer. "They have their own assignments. You'll go to Jamestown and continue your covert security training there until the rest of your team arrives."

"How long will that be?"

"I don't have that information," he said. "Their assignments are above my clearance level."

"Really?" She'd assumed that he knew everything about what was going on with her team.

"Why does that surprise you?" he asked.

"I don't know. I kind of thought you were our keeper, in a manner of speaking."

"I'm not," he said bluntly. "I'm your keeper, for exactly three more days. After that, you'll report directly to Admiral Krazinski. Whatever the other three are doing is not for me to know, and it won't be for you to know, either. Just as you won't be permitted to discuss this mission with them, they won't be able to discuss their assignments with you."

"But we're a team," she said. "Shouldn't we know what experiences the others have had?"

"Not this time," he said flatly.

"Is that how it was for your team?" she asked. "Did you have secrets from one another?"

He turned to her. "You'll always have secrets. Even from your team. That's what you signed up for, and that's how it will always be. Whatever happens here on Asimov, you won't speak of it. Whatever happens wherever they are, they won't speak of it. If you get split up again in the future, same thing. Your first duty is always to PAC command. Your second duty is to your team."

"That's not what you said before. You said that if I ever got caught in a situation where I had to choose between following orders and saving my team, I should save my team."

He let out a soft breath and his gaze dropped. She sensed he was reliving his past.

"That's life and death," he said. "And maybe I shouldn't have told you that."

"But if you could go back, you'd defy your orders in order to keep them alive, wouldn't you?"

"Yes."

"Why?" She kept her attention fixed on him, willing him to look up at her.

Finally, he did. "Because some things will break you, deep inside. Not in a way that anyone can see. In a way that, in time, maybe you can even ignore. Like losing an arm or a leg. As long as you focus on the limb you still have, you can avoid thinking about what's missing for a little while. But whenever things are too quiet, or too still, you'll remember how broken you really are."

He held her gaze and, for the first time, left his expression unguarded so that she could see the depth of his suffering.

She reached out and touched his hand. "You're not broken. You're still here. Strong. Smart. Funny. People love you as soon as they meet you. I can name three officers right now who are going to cry when you leave here."

"That's just my cover," he said. "It's not me."

"Then what's the real you? Is it how you are when you're with me?"

His gaze dropped as he considered, then his eyes met hers again. "I'm more of the real me than I've been since I lost my team. So thank you for that. I'm going to miss being assigned with you."

A sense of alarm rose in her. "Then stay. Let's campaign to have you join my team, just like I said earlier."

He shook his head. "You don't want that."

"I do."

"You're the leader of your team, but I'm senior to you. What's that going to do to your authority?"

"We'll figure it out," she said. "I don't care about that. My ego won't be hurt by sharing authority."

"It's too messy," he said. "Teams don't work that way."

"This one can," she insisted. "Or is it that you don't want to join my team? You've already had your team, and don't want to be part of mine?"

He smiled faintly. "That's not it. I like your team. I like you. If there were no other concerns, I'd be happy to be part of Avian Unit."

"Then let's make that happen," she said.

He simply looked at her, and she became aware that she was still touching him. She pulled her hands back, but he caught her fingers between his hands. "Wouldn't that be complicated?"

"No," she said automatically, but she knew she was lying. She had chemistry with him, and as of that moment, she was sure he had feelings for her. She had feelings for him, too, but they were different than what she felt for Raptor. And it wasn't in her nature to have those kinds of feelings for more than one person.

She pulled her hands free. "Maybe," she amended. "But what isn't complicated about being in Blackout? My team would be better with you, and as the leader, it's my job to advocate for what's best for my team. Unless you don't want to be part of Avian Unit, you should expect me to fight to have you stay with us."

Now empty, his hands curled loosely on the couch. He smiled. "All right. If you're sure, then who am I to argue with the leader of a Blackout unit?"

His response surprised her. She'd expected more argument. She eyed him cautiously. "Really?"

He smiled. A real smile. "Yeah. Life's messy. Complicated. We'll make it work as well as it can."

She smiled back. Maybe he was right, that it would be messy

and complicated, but that was what she expected from life. He needed a team and something to fill the void in him, and she knew her team would be better with him.

She felt a violent surge of something good. She was more than ready to be back with her team. And if Minho was with them, too, it would be worth whatever adjustments they had to make.

"Good. Now let's watch Lydecker like a hawk right up until the moment we leave this station," she said, turning back to the voicecom. "Today's the third day in his cycle. Tomorrow, we can watch his every move and see if we can figure out what he does every fourth day."

9

"I wish we could have put surveillance in Lydecker's quarters," Fallon frowned at the silent image of the captain as he receded down a corridor.

Tracking him in this manner was inefficient.

"Command was clear," Mino said. "Nothing out of the ordinary that he might discover. And if he were up to something bad, he'd be careful to watch such things, so it would only serve to let him know that someone was on to him. And if he's innocent, what do you think his reaction to such surveillance would be?"

"Not good."

"Yeah. Someone would have to take the fall for that. I sure don't want it to be me."

"Or me either, right?" she prompted.

"Eh. You're on your own, kid." He waited a couple of beats to let the humor hang in the air, then bumped her playfully with his shoulder. "Anyway, sometimes we're limited to relative basics like this. It's good practice for you. All the spy equipment is fun, and sure does help, but you can't rely on it to do your work for you."

"Do you think he's innocent?" she asked. "What are the odds

that we'll find something now, after not having found anything all this time?"

"Amount of time is irrelevant. Just because someone isn't doing shady shit today, it doesn't mean they won't be doing it tomorrow. Or next week."

"So basically, you consider everyone guilty until being caught at being guilty."

He smiled. "I like that. Yeah, that pretty much covers it. Everyone's guilty of something. It's just that most people are only guilty of unimportant things."

"If his pattern holds true," she said, watching the display in front of her, "he'll skip the mess hall."

A moment later, he boarded a lift and they waited to see what he selected for his destination.

"Deck Five," Fallon said in surprise. "Definitely not the mess hall, then, but why would he go to five?"

Minho frowned and shook his head.

She'd have to run back all prior security footage of each fourth day, checking Deck Five. Did he visit that same area each time or was this something new?

They watched him approach the seal-off point for the deck, then enter the heart of the containment system.

A tingle ran down Fallon's spine, like a drop of adrenaline charging up her backbone. This wasn't typical behavior. The captain had no reason to visit the containment system. Sure, it was his prerogative to visit any section on the station he chose to, and it wasn't impossible that he chose an unlikely place to visit every fourth morning, just to keep the crew on their toes.

But she didn't think so.

Judging from the tension she felt radiating from Minho, she didn't think he thought so, either.

Fallon checked the login details to see the last time someone had entered that area, and she realized that the captain wasn't alone. Someone else had entered just twenty minutes prior.

The zing of energy down her spine grew stronger.

"Priestley's in there," she murmured, her eyes glued to the view inside the containment unit.

"He must be outside of camera view," Minho said. "I can't find him in there."

They watched the captain advance into the area, move around a huge manifold, and pause.

"He must be there, taking physical readings," she said. "I'll see if that matches with the expected schedule.

She cross-referenced the master schedule of expected maintenance checks. "Yeah. That's due to be done today. Priestley's supposed to be there."

"But the captain isn't." Minho's eyes didn't leave the screen, though there was nothing to see. The captain's left shoulder and part of his back were visible, and he appeared to be looking downward.

Probably talking to Priestley.

"I wish we had audio," she muttered. Of course, that was against PAC's agreement among its member planets. Specific situations could warrant general audio recording, or could prompt short-term recording, but without probable cause, the privacy of PAC citizens was not to be impugned by excessive surveillance.

"What's so bad about having sensitive areas tapped for sound, anyway?" she asked. "It could provide important information in the event of a disaster."

"Audio recording happens automatically when an alert goes up. It's a slippery slope, to do constant surveillance, even in a sensitive area. That's why the matter is clearly addressed in the charter."

"Which Blackout breaks on a regular basis," she said.

"There are two levels of rules." Minho glanced at her briefly. "The ones that everyone understands as a given. Those give people a sense of expectation and safety, and they're for the betterment of the PAC as a whole. But then there's the other set of rules that people don't want to know about. The rules that govern the things that prove that their lives aren't as safe and protected as they think they are. Both have to exist. We need the populace to feel secure, and we need to be able to do the things that keep them that way. It may seem hypocritical to have two sets of rules that oppose each other, but in reality they work together for the same purpose."

"I know that," she said. "It's just strange to come to a crossroads between those two different sets of rules."

She saw movement on the screen. "Hang on. I think he's leaving."

Captain Lydecker turned smartly on his heel and left the same way he'd come.

"He doesn't look upset," Fallon ventured.

"No," Minho agreed. "He looks just as he did when he entered."

"So what did he and Priestley talk about?" she wondered. "It seems clear that Lydecker went there seeking Priestley out. He went directly in, spoke to him, and left without doing anything else."

Minho continued to watch the screen. Priestley came into view, carrying a diagnostic scanner.

"Two possibilities," Minho said. "Either Lydecker and Priestley have always been in league with each other, or the captain wants to coerce him into something."

She'd thought the same thing. "Lydecker's been feigning disapproval for Priestley to throw people off."

"Maybe," Minho said. "Or he wanted to increase pressure on Priestley. To flex his authority and push Priestley toward desperation."

"Which wouldn't be too hard," Fallon realized. "Since Priestley doesn't have any fallback. No place to go back to. No people to rely on. He's the perfect mark."

"Exactly. But now the question is, what is he the mark for? And we've got another problem."

They looked at each other in understanding.

She said what they were both thinking. "We only have two days to figure out what the captain's doing and gather the proof because if we were to stay here longer, he'd be instantly suspicious."

They had their work cut out for them.

At lunchtime, Fallon sent a message to Priestley, casually suggesting he drop by her quarters after his shift. She didn't want to arouse the captain's suspicion by doing anything out of the ordinary.

She didn't invite Minho, both to keep the meeting lowkey and not noteworthy to any observers, and to keep Priestley at ease. She sensed that he'd be more comfortable with just her.

She really needed him to put all his trust in her. If what she suspected was happening was truly happening, Priestley would be faced with choosing between her and the captain. She had to make sure he chose her.

If she screwed this up, she and Minho would lose their advantage of operating in secret. The entire thing would become a showdown, and that would only make this bigger and more harmful to bystanders.

When he arrived, he looked curious but not suspicious. He'd only been to her quarters once before, but she wanted him to know that they were speaking in a private place. She and Minho both checked their quarters every time they returned to them to make sure no surveillance devices had been installed. She knew that Lydecker had no eyes or ears inside her quarters, but she couldn't be so sure about Priestley's quarters.

"Hey, Emiko," he said as he entered and the doors closed behind him. "What's up?"

She gestured to the couch. "Have a seat."

She'd debated on what approach to take. Pretending to know more than she did seemed like the best method, so she took a breath and sat.

"As you know," she began, "I'm here on behalf of PAC command to fulfill a security role. It's come to my attention that there's a security breach in progress on Asimov. I wanted to talk to you about this personally, and in private, to see if there's anything you can tell me."

He paled and his eyes widened slightly. "A security breach? No, I don't know anything about that. Why would you think I do? My clearance is the lowest clearance possible while still having access to the areas I need to work on."

She folded her hands in her lap. "I'm pretty sure that when I say that this is something that goes quite far up the chain of command, you might have a suspicion about what I mean. I need you to tell me about that suspicion, in detail."

She paused and looked at him pointedly, but he remained frozen. If this went wrong, this situation was going to get ugly, fast. She continued, "I know you, and you know me. I also know the risk I'm asking you to take. If you help me, I can protect you."

His hands clenched together in his lap. His eyes looked like there was a war going on behind them.

Time to put all her cards on the table. "I know he's the captain, but I have a great deal of influence of my own. There's a reason I'm a security specialist. I also have authoritative power that exceeds my rank when it comes to security issues. Now, I need you to decide. Are you going to tell me what you know?"

He looked like he wanted to run. She prepared herself to tackle him if he did. Whatever happened, she couldn't let him get to Lydecker and warn him.

"He said…" Priestley's voice came out in a rasp. He cleared his throat and started again. "He said if I didn't follow his orders, he'd make sure no one, anywhere, ever hired me."

"Who?" She needed him to say it out loud.

"Captain Lydecker." Priestley stared at his hands.

"What does he want you to do?"

"There's a delivery arriving in two days. I'm supposed to log into the system to receive it, then get lost."

"Get lost?" Fallon repeated.

"Not verify the contents of the shipment or monitor its unloading. Take a walk while it's being handled."

"Why?"

Priestley shook his head. "He said it's standard on stations. That there were classified transactions that couldn't go on record."

"Did that sound right to you?" she asked. "Legit?"

"No, but he's the captain and what do I know? Plus, I need the job. He disliked me from the beginning. I think he'd be more than glad to get rid of me."

"I don't think so," she said. "I think his dislike is manufactured. He's been grooming you since the first time he met you. Teaching you to fear him and reinforcing the power differential between you. It's a classic way of exploiting someone."

"For what, though?" Priestley asked. "Contraband? Smuggling?"

"I don't know," Fallon said. "But we're going to find out in two days."

THE TIMING WOULD BE TRICKY. Minho and Fallon were scheduled to leave in two days, which also happened to be when Captain Lydecker's mysterious package would arrive.

A message to Admiral Krazinski ensured that the transport

was delayed just enough to give it an ETA at the very end of that day.

Now they just needed to hope that whatever Lydecker was bringing to Asimov didn't get delayed.

They didn't bring Katheryn in on what they were doing. The fewer people who knew anything was going on, the better. Fallon and Minho kept a close watch on Priestley. They didn't think he'd go to Lydecker, but they couldn't just trust that he wouldn't, either.

Ironically, amidst the belief that the captain of the station was engaging in some sort of illegal behavior, they officially signed off on the station's security the day before their scheduled departure.

Yeah, sure, everything was ship-shape, perfectly fine. Nothing out of the ordinary at all.

The ideal versus reality reminded her of what Minho had said about there being things that most people were better off not knowing.

They watched everything closely, obsessing over every detail and being careful to look like they were doing everything just as one would expect a couple of officers with no official duties to do.

The night before the arrival of the transport, she stayed in Minho's quarters.

"Won't that look a little..." She raised her eyebrows suggestively when he told her to sleep over.

"Exactly," he confirmed. "Half the crew thinks we're an item anyway. We'll just be furthering the idea that we're enjoying some recreational time when, really, we're making sure we can't be ambushed separately."

"All right." She'd shrugged. "But I get the bed."

He rolled his eyes slightly. "Don't be childish. We'll both sleep in the bed. That's the point of not being separated. I know you've slept in the same bed with Hawk. This will be like that."

"We were drunk," she grumbled. "Besides, Hawk and I..." she

trailed off, realizing she didn't want to say what she'd been about to say.

She and Hawk had no attraction for each other whatsoever. She might as well be sleeping next to a big, snoring boulder as alongside Hawk.

However, she didn't want to give Minho the idea that she felt differently about him. Because she didn't. Nope. This would be just like sleeping in Hawk's quarters.

That night, they locked themselves in the quarters, triggered the outer door, then triggered the door to the bedroom. Anyone attempting to enter without the passcode would get a nasty shock.

"Cute trick," Fallon said.

"Thanks. It's nice for when you want to get some sleep, but don't want someone sawing off your head while you do it."

She laughed.

He smiled. "Not many people would laugh at that."

"I guess we share a sense of humor."

The overnight bag she'd brought, setting at the bottom right corner of the bed, caught her eye. She willed herself to be cool about the situation. It was a stakeout. A weird one, but just a work thing.

"I guess I'll get ready for bed then," she said. "For sleep," she amended, then regretted having done so.

She ducked into the necessary with her bag and closed the door.

"Ack!" Minho wore a wide-eyed look when Fallon emerged from the necessary, clean, wet-haired, and wearing long lounge pants with a short-sleeved shirt.

"Nothing." He stood up and stepped around the bed to the necessary, closing the door.

She sat on the bed. *Ack*? She looked at herself, looking for a tear in her pajamas or a stain or something.

Everything looked fine.

When he emerged fifteen minutes later, she sat at the head of the bed on the side closer to the necessary. His long pants and short-sleeved shirt were almost identical to hers except for color and size.

"Why did you say 'ack' before?" she demanded.

He ran his fingers through his damp hair. "Well, I saw that you hadn't dressed to impress. You looked a bit frumpy, to be honest. I've gotten used to seeing you in your uniform. Forget I said it."

"You're wearing the same thing!" she exclaimed.

He patted his shirt with his palms. "I feel like I bring a little extra something to this ensemble."

"I'm not seeing it."

"Look closer." He put his hands on his hips.

"Nope. Nothing."

"Really?" He pursed his lips in puzzlement. "Well, clearly you don't know greatness when you see it. That's just as well, though, given the circumstances."

He made a general gesture at the room, the station, and them.

She laughed. She shouldn't have worried. In all the time she'd known him, she'd never known Minho to be unable to handle whatever came at him. She should have known he would handle this, too.

It kind of did feel like one of her sleepovers with Hawk now. They laughed together a lot, too.

He stood at the edge of the bed and started to sit down, then drew back. "Ah, I almost forgot. Rules for the night. Keep your hands and feet to yourself. No kicking, no punching, and absolutely *no* pillow stealing. I'm serious, I'll get mad about that one. If you snore, I reserve the right to shake your shoulder vigorously and possibly call you a jerk."

He pulled back the blanket and sat.

"Anything else?" she asked.

He gazed upward thoughtfully. "If you're the type who gets up to go pee, I advise you do it quietly. I might think you're an assassin and take you down."

"Noted." She grabbed the blanket and pulled it up to her knees.

"What, you have no conditions?" he asked.

"I think the same ones you said will do just fine."

He nodded. "Okay. Except for the snoring thing. These are my quarters, and if I snore, that's just my privilege."

She arched an eyebrow and said nothing. Maybe that was what he thought.

"Ready for lights out?" he asked. "We have a long day tomorrow."

"We do," she agreed. "Hopefully we'll get everything here sorted so we can move on."

"I've never known anything to be that simple, but okay, we'll hope for that." He turned the light down to only five percent illumination, darkening the room without leaving it pitch black and leaving her to lie awake thinking about what he'd said.

Fallon's eyes snapped open. She'd heard something. She stayed perfectly still, listening.

Then she realized that Minho's face was only centimeters away.

Right. There was a reason she'd felt like she wasn't alone—because she wasn't.

The faint light silhouetted his cheek, forehead, and nose. His breathing was slow and even.

She watched him, careful not to make any noise.

There was no point in denying that she liked him. She liked

him a lot. For multiple reasons, she couldn't reach out and touch his cheek.

She'd never do that to Raptor. She'd never do that to her team, either, because surely whatever happened between her and Raptor would have some fallout on Avian Unit.

That kind of selfishness had no room in her life.

Very slowly and carefully, she edged backward, putting more space between them. She closed her eyes, listening to his breathing for a long time before she fell back to sleep.

Fallon opened her eyes to find Minho staring at her.

"You're awake," he said.

"Either that or I'm creepy as hell, sleeping with my eyes open." She pulled back and sat at the edge of the bed.

He rolled over and sat up, too. "I'm going with awake. Though I don't deny you can be creepy, too."

She checked the time. "Scrap."

"Okay, two things," he said. "First, you need to learn some grown-up swear words. You're in covert ops now. You just had a good opportunity to say, 'Prelin's ass!' and passed it up."

"And the second thing?" she asked, amused.

"Right. What made you say 'scrap?'"

"A gentle upbringing, perhaps. Hawk's been a bad influence on me and I do swear more these days, but I guess I need to work harder."

He laughed. "No, I meant, what's wrong?"

She knew what he'd meant, but pretended otherwise. "It's too early to go do anything. The day shift hasn't even started."

"Right. And it would probably look odd for us not to take a leisurely start to the day. So we have a couple of hours in here together. Whatever shall we do?" He leaned back against the bulkhead of the bedroom and gave her a slow smile.

A slow, wicked smile.

She felt like she'd been flash-frozen, then dropped into a deep fryer.

"Breakfast?" She wasn't sure where the word came from, but, sure, that was a reasonable thing for her to say.

He snapped his fingers, then pointed at her. "Exactly. I have a fair bit of stuff in the kitchenette. We might as well make something good. I love how in sync we are."

He gave her that smile again. It wasn't a regular smile. It was a smile that said things that his words didn't.

He was teasing her. They both knew there was something between them, and they both knew nothing was going to happen. So he was joking about it.

That jerk! Her tension about the situation eased and she laughed. "Perfect. You go get started. I'll pull my hair back and be in there in a few minutes."

AFTER COOKING everything Minho had in his kitchenette and eating more than she usually did in a single meal, the day shift started and Fallon and Minho ventured out.

Today they would be like tourists, or officers enjoying some shore leave. They'd poke around the station under the guise of taking a little vacation time between the completion of their duties here and the next assignment that awaited them.

Wearing casual clothes rather than their uniforms, they strolled along the station's boardwalk. Almost all of the commercial spaces had been claimed by colorful shops and fragrant eateries. Fallon also noticed a beauty treatment boutique, an open-air meat-stick vendor, and no fewer than three pubs.

"That's a lot of pubs for one space station," Fallon noted to Minho after they passed the third.

"You don't know," he said. "Maybe that's essential to live here after a year or two."

She laughed. Despite everything, she was having fun. That worked well, since she was supposed to appear to be enjoying some leisure time. She'd have expected to have a ball of tension in her stomach, waiting for Lydecker's transport to arrive, but somehow, whenever the stakes got higher, she always felt more vital and ebullient.

"Oh look," he said. "It's the girly shop."

"The what?" She followed his gaze to the boutique with a pretty window that displayed perfumes, jeweled hair clips, and frilly underpinnings. "Oh, right."

He edged in front of her to stop her from moving on. "We should go in."

"No, we really shouldn't. Unless that kind of thing appeals to you. Because it's doesn't to me."

"Sure, sure," he said dismissively. "We both know you're all killer instinct and blood and guts or whatever. But all the people who are watching us without letting on that they're watching us think they're seeing a couple doing a little fun shopping together. We should go in, for the cover."

She narrowed her eyes at him. "I don't believe you. You just want to get me in there so you can laugh at how much those things don't suit me."

"Never. I'm a professional. It's for the cover." He wore a totally believable look of sincerity.

She didn't believe it. "Fine. Five minutes. Then I get to pick the next place."

He nodded, smiling. "Whatever you say, dear."

"Don't do that."

"Okay," he agreed quickly. "I am officially not doing that."

She stiffened her spine and stepped into the shop. On closer inspection, she saw that it had décor, too. Feathery fronds tucked into shiny vases lined one display shelf.

"Those are nice," Minho said, looking at them.

"I've never been much for knick knacks," she said. "Even if I were, it's not like I'd want to lug that kind of thing from assignment to assignment."

"I didn't say I was going to buy you one," he said defensively. "I just said they were nice."

"Okay. They're nice." She eyed him suspiciously. She didn't trust him not to pull some kind of shenanigans like saddling her with some useless object she didn't want.

The shopkeep wandered over, welcomed them, then subtly drifted away, remaining in the background so that she wasn't hovering over them while remaining available for inquiries.

Fallon admired her deftness. "She's good."

"Of course she is. Not just anyone can get approval to own a shop on a PAC station. Only the most professional, most ethical businesspeople."

"Right." He seemed to be in an odd, perky mood. Maybe it was just part of the act. Maybe he was looking forward to wrapping up this mission.

They browsed around, made some appropriately admiring comments, then ducked back out.

"Your choice now," he said.

"There." Fallon pointed at the dry goods store.

"Really? I thought you'd be looking for something I wouldn't like." He seemed mildly disappointed.

"No matter what I chose, you wouldn't care, so I might as well go someplace I'd actually like to see." Without waiting to see if he was following, she hurried over and entered the shop.

"Mm." She took a long, deep breath. "It smells good in here."

"Real wood," Minho said, also breathing in. "Not the synthetic stuff. It's one of the best smells in the galaxy."

"It is, isn't it?" She kept taking deep lungfuls of it. Enclosed spaces like stations and ships never had this organic sort of fragrance. They always had a very dry, almost antiseptic smell.

"Were you looking for something in particular?" Minho asked

as they admired hand-carved tables displaying leather wallets and bags of all sizes, wooden display boxes, wooden carvings, and more.

"Tea," she said, kneeling down to touch a large box on the floor. "This is beautiful."

Apparently that was the shopkeep's signal, because he chose that moment to approach them. "That's one of my favorite pieces that just came in on the last delivery."

The middle-aged human smiled and bent down next to her, running a hand over the lid. "This is all carved from two single pieces, lid and bottom. See? No seams."

He tapped the gently rounded corners on the outside of the container. "And inside, you'll see it's lined with priyanomine, so it's as secure as anything you'll find. Beautiful and secure. That's pretty nice, in my book."

"It really is beautiful," Fallon said. She'd been thinking she could use it for her knife collection, which had grown recently, but the priyanomine lining certainly put it out of her price range, even without having to ask.

She straightened. "I actually came for tea. Do you have it?"

The man nodded and straightened. "Of course. Many varieties from across the PAC, and some outside of it. Are you looking for just the tea, or do you need a case for it?"

Now that he mentioned it, a container for a tea stash she could take with her from place to place would be useful. "What do you have?"

He showed her a variety of tea boxes at a range of prices. Her favorite was a dark, polished-wood box that was on the pricey side, but not exorbitant. Since it was a useful item she intended to use for a very long time, it seemed worth it. "I'll take this one, with a variety of black and herbal teas, please."

Minho tapped a slightly larger, lighter-colored box. "This one's nice, too."

She smirked. He wasn't subtle. But he'd helped her so much,

from teaching her how to be a blackout officer to being able to doctor up food packets. "And that one too, for my little friend here," she said.

The shopkeep smiled broadly and went to bring out his tea offerings.

"Are you buying me a present?" Minho asked.

"Looks like it," she agreed.

"Aw. You shouldn't have."

"You practically begged me to." She arched an eyebrow at him.

He merely smiled.

They selected their tea, organized it neatly into the boxes, and Fallon paid for it all. She pretended to be put out about it, but she didn't truly mind.

Though she hoped to convince PAC command to assign Minho to her team, she had no reason to think it would happen. If it didn't, her time with him was drawing to a close, and she didn't know when she'd see him again. Buying him a gift seemed like a good thing to do.

"What now?" she asked.

"Hm, what time is it?" Minho checked his chronometer and said, "It's about lunchtime."

She shook her head. "I'm still full from breakfast."

"So am I, actually. What about getting some coffee and sitting on the boardwalk to people watch?"

"Sure," she said. "That seems nice and conspicuous. Nope, we couldn't possibly be planning something if we're just wasting time sitting around, right?"

He nudged her with his elbow, smiling. "Something like that."

It was funny to count down the hours before something big by doing the most inconsequential of things. Being in Blackout meant a lot of incongruities and conflicting extremes. She hadn't quite gotten used to the murkiness of operating within hidden spaces yet.

Still, it was their job to appear to be entirely focused on themselves—or each other—while paying no attention at all to the transport that was drawing ever closer to Asimov.

What was on it? Admiral Krazinski had given no indication at all as to what Lydecker might be dealing in. Was Lydecker serving as a way station to broker stolen goods between merchant and buyer? That would certainly be something a captain could do. Or maybe he was hiding a front that took PAC-issued goods and pilfered them to private buyers. He had the authority to make a scam like that work, too.

Whatever it was, it had to be lucrative. It had to be something worth risking his commission as a captain for.

Worth the risk of being imprisoned, too.

"You look serious all of a sudden," Minho said.

She looked down at the lukewarm coffee she hadn't wanted to drink. "Just mentally taking stock. Preparing for what comes next."

"Have you ever been to Sarkan?" he asked suddenly.

"No. I haven't been much of anywhere yet."

"When you get a chance," he said, "take a vacation there. Especially if things have been rough."

"Why?"

"It's beautiful there. Clean air, lots of beaches, and the people, on the whole, are the nicest you'll find anywhere. Non-judgmental, kind, and welcoming. It's the perfect place to go when you start to think the universe must be full of nothing but terrible people."

Aha, so this line of conversation did have a point, after all.

"Sounds nice. I'll be sure to visit there sometime."

They remained there long after she'd gotten bored, simply for the purpose of making their whereabouts known, and showing that they were doing nothing but killing time. Minho kept the conversation light, but she was tired of waiting. She wanted to finally take care of what they'd been sent there to do.

"I've had it with your mistakes!" A loud voice rang out, making Fallon shift to see what was happening.

A tall woman shoved a shorter, much younger woman. "Always costing me money. I took you on as a charity, and you do nothing but get in my way. Well, I'm done. Find your own way off this station."

The woman started to stomp away, but the younger woman caught her arm. "Then where's my pay for the past month? You're not leaving without giving it to me."

The older woman snarled. "Oh, I'll give you something."

She hurled herself at the younger woman and they went down in a pile of fists and shrieks.

Minho and Fallon eyed each other. They stood, but remained on the fringes as three men arrived and waded into the fray.

Now people were shouting and hurrying, either away from the area to get out of harm's way or toward it to get a better look at the spectacle.

Security arrived within minutes, pulling people apart, shouting orders for people to move along, and trying to restore order.

When the scene had been cleared, gawkers remained, exclaiming their shock over having witnessed such a scene. Officers returned to their posts, but visitors to the station took pleasure in expressing their horror.

"Did you see that?" Minho asked in a low voice, as the confusion calmed.

"Yep." While everyone else had been watching the people fighting, she'd been watching everything else.

"It's begun," Minho said. "There are more people involved with this than we realized."

The two of them went to the security officer to offer their help, but were, of course, thanked and sent on their way.

"Let's go," Minho said as they left, heading back toward their quarters. "We're all in now."

10

THE BEAUTY of having installed a security system was being able to become a ghost.

Fallon, wearing a snug black shirt and pants, proceeded through the guts of the station via service conduits. No one would detect her, and nothing would record her.

Over a private channel locked down to only his end and hers, Minho said, "Report."

"Almost there," she said. "No concerns."

"Good. I'm in position and monitoring all hot spots."

"Acknowledged. Stand by."

Gone was their humor and banter. They were all business now.

She arrived at her destination—a conduit nexus above Docking Bay Seven, where the transport was scheduled to arrive. After setting out her VR gear, she took a flat display out of the bag she'd been dragging along with her.

Unfolding the display, she connected it to all the surveillance points she'd called up earlier.

At least two of the shopkeeps were in on Lydecker's operation, whatever it was. She and Minho had witnessed that first-hand when the distraction on the boardwalk had gone down. There had been no mistaking their lack of surprise, or how much they had lent to the confusion with their shouting and flailing.

Plus, of course, the actors creating the distraction were part of it.

She wondered who else. Was anyone on the security staff involved, or had the distraction been designed only to keep them temporarily preoccupied? And how had all of this been orchestrated so quickly after Asimov's being brought into service?

The only possible explanation was that this was an existing collaboration that had been going on for some time, and simply transferred over to Asimov.

In that moment, she realized that there was a lot more work to do on this than just what would happen that day. This was far from over.

What did that mean for her and Avian Unit? What did it mean for her and Minho?

She saw the captain on the move and pushed those thoughts away.

"Lydecker's leaving ops control," she told Minho. "Headed toward section E, but I don't know if that's his destination."

"Keep an eye on him," Minho said. "Watch that docking bay, too. We have everything recording to an independent device in case he wipes it later, but we need to know who we're dealing with and how outnumbered we are."

There were two of them and a dozen or more of the smugglers. Not the most auspicious odds, but Minho and Fallon had prepared with the time and resources that were available to them.

All they had to do was collect the evidence and get it to PAC command. Once that was done, the guilty could be apprehended and dealt with, and their associates would be discovered.

It sure sounded simple.

"Minho, he's gotten on a lift. He's headed to Deck Three."

"Watch him. Do *not* lose him. Maintain an open channel. I'm on the move."

She heard him mutter some curse words.

Deck Three housed lower-level officers. Other than the crew quarters, it had only one noteworthy feature. The captain's trajectory confirmed her suspicion.

"He's going to crisis ops," she told Minho.

"Not good," Minho said, "but it's what I expected."

Every station had a crisis ops control. Should the main ops control be damaged, the crisis section could control the entire station, or even function independently of it.

It was also incredibly hard to break into, since it had been designed to be the last vestige in the worst of crisis situations. If a command crew wanted to make itself inaccessible, that would be the place to go.

That couldn't be what Lydecker was after, though. As of yet, he had no reason to think anything was amiss.

"He's going to give that transport permissions it shouldn't have, isn't he?" Fallon asked Minho over the open channel.

"Pretty sure." Minho's voice sounded slightly strained and she imagined him crawling through a conduit up a ladder.

"Its ETA is still on target," she reported. "It already has permission to dock. Ten minutes."

Would the captain remain in crisis ops that entire time? Probably. That way, he could quietly cover everything up and return to ops control as if he'd simply taken a brief meeting or visited the necessary.

Was this his first time doing this kind of thing, or was it the first time he had the opportunity to do something on this scale?

"He's in," she reported.

"Almost there." Minho sounded like he was gritting his teeth.

"Door's closed," she said. "I'd bet he's activated a security seal."

"But I'll be nearby, in case something goes down here. Otherwise, I'll meet you at the rendezvous point. Just give me the countdown."

"If something does happen and you go out in the open, be careful," she warned. "All those cameras are live, and Lydecker and his people might be watching."

"Yeah. Lots of question marks here."

"Yeah," she echoed.

A note of concern entered his voice. "You okay?"

"Fine. I just wish we were better prepared. Or had more people on our side. Or something."

"Nature of the job. You'll get used to it. Can you see anything he's doing in there?"

She checked all the readouts she had running on rapid rotation. "No. Wait. Docking Bay Seven's surveillance feed just stopped recording."

"Is the backup still going?"

"Yes." She checked the drone that she'd parked in the bay. "All good."

She checked the incoming transport ship. It was a small one—the kind a station might see a dozen times a day if it were on a heavily trafficked flight path. Just a freelancer with cargo to unload. Those ships were usually the most tightly regulated, given that they had no larger company or PAC association.

"Anything going on there?" Fallon asked. "The ship's on approach."

"Not a thing. Let me know when it begins docking and I'll make my way to you."

"Understood." On sensors, she watched the little ship align itself with the station, adopt a synchronous rotation, and lock into the docking clamps.

"It's here. No clearance to board yet. Any second."

"On my way. Don't do anything crazy before I get there," he joked.

At least, she thought he was being funny. Maybe not.

"I'll try my best but can't promise," she answered. She wasn't sure if she meant it or not, either. She'd have to wait and see.

As the minutes passed, she wasn't sure which would arrive first—the transport or Minho. The airlock was pressurizing when she heard bumping and scuffling.

"I sure hope that's you," she said over the still-open channel between them.

"Funny." He crawled into view, dragging a bag behind him, and switched the channel off. "Are they here?"

"Any minute."

He sat on his knees next to her, watching the monitor.

A pair of men came through the airlock, then another man and a woman. They took a look around the docking bay, conferred, then the first two men walked out onto the boardwalk.

Did that mean they had nothing to deliver? If so, then they were there to onboard something.

"Track that one," Minho said.

The man wouldn't have access to anything but Deck One. At least, he shouldn't.

"No movement from Lydecker," Fallon noted. Thus far, the captain had remained in crisis ops.

On Deck One, surveillance was plentiful, as opposed to more personal areas like living quarters. It was easy to watch the visitor make his way along the boardwalk, continuing past everything without pause until he got to the second pub.

"Seems a little early for a drink," Minho observed dryly. "He just got here."

"The bartender on duty there is one of the ones who was there earlier, during the brawl," Fallon said. "I doubt that's a coincidence. I wish I could go follow him and see what's going on in there."

The pub had no cameras inside.

"We need to stay where we are, unless there's a really good reason not to," he said. "We're not here to stop anything. We're here to get proof and deliver it to Krazinski. With just the two of us here, it's all we can really do without blowing our cover. It's not like we can low-key commandeer the station."

"Yeah. Too bad. That'd make a great story."

He smirked at her.

They saw the man emerge from the bar and reverse course, back toward their location. Two of his colleagues paced around the docking bay, stretching their arms and backs, while one of them had gone back onto their ship.

Though Fallon had audio recording enabled on the drone, it hadn't caught any useful conversation.

The tall man returned to the docking bay. After the doors closed behind him, he nodded to the man and woman waiting for him.

Fallon saw their shoulders relax and the three of them turned back to the ship.

"Wait," Fallon said. "That's not it…is it?'

Docking Bay Seven sent a request for departure.

"New plan," Minho said. "We're going with them. Send all this to Krazinski on a secure channel as quickly as you can, and then follow me."

Without waiting for her acknowledgement, he hurried back the way he'd come.

Fallon crammed all the surveillance they'd done into an open channel, and downloaded it to a local device too, which she removed and slipped into her belt. The rest of the gear would have to stay here.

She took off after Minho.

He'd already aborted the depressurization of the airlock and was inputting kill codes to force it open.

"You ready?" He looked at her as it opened.

"Yeah."

"Good," he said. "I killed their communication with the station. Now get that ship open."

Her? She'd thought he would do it, since this was a pressure situation. She didn't hesitate, though, and used Asimov's link and her security clearance to access the ship's hatch.

In less than a minute, they forced their way onto the ship and ran toward its bridge.

A man and a woman ran to stop them.

The narrow corridor didn't leave a lot of space for fighting, so Fallon grabbed the woman and yanked her close to give Minho space to move forward and face off against the guy.

The woman wasn't much of a fighter. She tried to grapple Fallon to take her down, but Fallon easily slipped from her grasp.

Since it seemed unsporting to hit her more than necessary, Fallon delivered a moderate punch to the woman's stomach, and when she was doubled over, Fallon forced her to the ground. With the woman on her knees, Fallon reached to her back and removed a set of zip cuffs, securing the woman's wrists around her back.

Minho's opponent was putting up more of a fight, but he didn't have much more skill than his partner huddled on the floor.

With a quick right hook, Minho connected with the guy's temple and knocked him out. As he fell, Minho grabbed him to ease his landing, then cuffed his arms behind his back.

"Where should we stick them?" he asked.

Fallon consulted the schematic of the ship she'd glanced at while waiting for it to dock.

"There's no good location," she said. "All the rooms that close off with doors will have voicecoms they could use."

"Where's the closest conduit or emergency ladder?" he asked.

"One section forward, starboard side."

"Grab her." Minho nodded toward the woman as he grabbed the man by the feet and dragged him down the corridor.

In the emergency ladder, he used another set of zip cuffs to attach them both to the wall via the cuffs they already wore. They could either stand or let their arms hang above their heads. Either way, they weren't going to be very comfortable. The man was awake and sitting up when Fallon and Minho descended the ladder, heading for the bridge.

"Here." Fallon pulled open an access panel and climbed in, leading Minho toward a place that would allow them to drop into the bridge from above rather than try to get through the door. If their presence on the ship was known, surely the other two crew members would be waiting for that.

They didn't have any time to waste.

"There's no way to do this quietly," she said when she had her hands on the access panel above the bridge.

"Then do it loud and fast. You drop in first, while they're surprised. I'll be right behind you."

She took a deep breath, tensed all of her muscles, and wrenched the panel off, throwing it free in the same movement. Immediately, she slid forward, dangled her legs down, gripped the edge of the opening, and lowered herself down.

She dropped two meters, landing on bent legs with only a small stumble. The impact of the landing radiated up her body even as she turned with her fists up to the tall man who had visited the boardwalk.

"What is this?" he shouted. "Who are you?"

She intended to answer him with a punch to his throat, but he deflected the blow and her fist glanced over his shoulder as he twisted away.

She heard Minho behind her, but didn't take her eyes off the tall guy.

"Did Missiny send you?" he asked.

"Yeah," she agreed. "He's pissed."

"It wasn't me," the man said.

Fallon noticed his hand going to his waist. He had a weapon. A stinger, probably. Too bad. They were the least interesting way to fight.

On the other hand, she didn't have one because she hadn't wanted it to be picked up by any passive sensors, so that made things a little more interesting.

She found talking and fighting at the same time kind of fun, and since it might distract him, she thought she'd keep going with it. "I'm pissed, too."

Moving in while his hand was on his belt, she grabbed his elbow, yanked it back at his shoulder blade, and brought her foot down on the back of his left knee.

He dropped and she went with him, her hand grasping for the stinger he'd been trying to reach.

He had his fist wrapped around it. He couldn't get it off his belt, but neither could she. And she couldn't let go of that hand or he'd get control of the stinger and this would be all over.

Using her body weight, she pressed down on him, keeping her hand clenched over his. She heard Minho squaring off with the other guy but couldn't spare them a glance. She used her left hand to reach for her own belt, and pulled out a small knife, which she jammed into the man's wrist. His hand went slack and she grabbed the stinger, pointing it at him and backing away.

She didn't need him awake right now, so she checked the stinger settings, then gave him a blast to knock him unconscious. She slapped some zip cuffs on him.

One down, one to go.

She turned to Minho and his opponent, but Minho already had him on the ground and was zip cuffing him.

"Him too," Minho said. "He can only cause us trouble right now."

With a careful shot, she knocked him unconscious, too.

Minho stood up and looked at her. "Is that your blood?"

She looked at her hand, which was coated in it. "No. His."

He nodded. "Good. You can slap a bandage on him and keep an eye on these two while I get us out of here. Once we get some distance, we'll see what they know."

He sat at the helm.

"I don't see an emergency med kit anywhere." She prowled the bridge, looking in all the likely places.

"Probably doesn't have one. Make do." He spoke to her tersely, his eyes on the voicecom.

The ship's bridge wasn't exactly brimming with makeshift bandage materials. The only real options were the clothes the four of them were wearing, and the one the tall guy wore already had a fair bit of blood on it.

She wasn't inclined to use her own shirt for him, either.

Instead, she went to the guy's crew mate, and cut his shirt off him, then fashioned it tightly around the wounded man's wrist.

It would have to do for now.

On second thought, she wiped her bloody hand off on the wounded man's pant leg. Sure, it probably added insult to injury, but she was low on options.

Keeping an eye on their captives, she joined Minho at the helm. Standing over his shoulder, she asked, "Does Asimov know anything's happened?"

"I don't think so. I'm not seeing any alerts, and they haven't contacted the ship other than to acknowledge the intention to depart."

"So as far as anyone there knows, everything went according to plan?" Fallon barely dared to hope it could be true.

"Until they realize we're not on board. I think they'll figure something out pretty fast," he said.

Fallon wondered how long that would take. "Then our first priority is getting enough distance from them that they won't find us when they come looking."

"Exactly. Let's see how fast this ship can go."

"Move over."

He glanced up at her. "What?"

"If you want to squeeze all the power we can from of this bucket, you should let me handle it."

He smiled suddenly. "You're right. And also, that was really cool the way you said that."

She laughed. "This is a strange time for compliments."

"If not now, then when?" He got up and gestured grandly to the seat. "For all we know, we'll get blown up by some crony of these guys, and this will be my last chance to say something flattering."

"Oh, nice," she said sarcastically. She spared him a look of disgust before focusing all of her attention on the ship's systems and how she could bleed out as much power as possible without damaging the propulsion system too significantly.

Minho went to check on the captives. "They'll be waking up before long. I'll go clear some quarters so they can't make trouble and stow them there. I'll also make absolutely certain there are no other surprises on board."

"Good," she said distractedly.

"Stay aware while I'm gone, just in case," he said.

"Hardly needs to be said." Like she was going to get so lost in what she was doing that she missed the baddie holding a pipe over her head until it was too late. This wasn't a holo-vid.

"I know," he said as he got to the door. "But I'd rather regret saying something than regret not saying something."

"I thought you were going," she said.

He left the bridge.

FALLON GAZED at the pea-sized sphere.

It was strange to think that the past several months of her life had been for this.

It was stranger to think that this tiny little lump could have destroyed all of Asimov Station, had it been activated.

However, its reveal had explained why Captain Lydecker would risk his career and his freedom.

The promise of unimaginable wealth had a way of seducing people into taking terrible risks.

"How much do you suppose this is worth?" Fallon asked Minho. The sphere was nestled inside a soft lining, which had been secured in a small priyanomine box that could fit in a person's pocket.

The presence of the priyanomine had made her laugh. There was a certain ridiculousness in encasing something so volatile in something that couldn't hope to contain it that struck her as terribly funny.

"More than you and I will ever make in our lives, that's for sure." Minho knelt next to her and peered at the sphere. "I've never seen brivinium in person."

"Probably because it's all supposed to be on Briv, and even among the Briveen, I bet few people have been in the same room with it."

"True," he agreed. "They probably stow it all away in some insane underground bunker." He paused. "It's kind of pretty."

It did have a shiny, iridescent quality that reminded her of Briveen scales. Though it was mostly an oily dark gray, if she moved her head one way or the other, she could see an emerald green hue moving across the surface.

"At least these idiots didn't try to deny knowing what it is," Fallon said, tilting her head to indicate the four captives who remained imprisoned in the quarters next door, which Minho had fashioned into a makeshift brig.

"Actually," Minho countered, "it could have been kind of amusing to watch them try."

She smiled. "I guess. But what do we do with it? We can't exactly take it back to Jamestown. Or anywhere within the vicinity of life of any kind."

Brivinium wasn't particularly volatile, until it was detonated. But it only took a very small explosion to do that. A mere projectile bullet could do it.

"Yeah, there's a good reason the PAC has banned this stuff for anywhere but the Briveen home planet. I've called for a rendezvous with a ship that will switch places with us. They'll take this ship and its crew to be dealt with, and we'll continue in the other ship to deliver this to the Briveen."

"To Briv itself, or will someone meet us and take it? Because I'd like to share living space with this thing for as little time as possible." She raised her forefinger and extended it toward the sphere.

"You're complaining about being near it, but you're going to touch it?" he asked, amused.

"Touching it can't do anything," she said. It was true. She knew it was true. But there was a long, deep chasm that divided academic knowledge and a gut feeling.

Her gut told her not to touch it.

She lowered the finger.

He grinned at her hesitation. "I haven't gotten anything back from command yet, so I don't know how we'll hand it off."

"Maybe they're busy arresting Lydecker," she suggested. She tried to imagine what was happening on Asimov.

"We can hope. Since there was no senior staff in the vicinity. Orders will have to be given for Lydecker's own crew to take him into custody. That's awfully messy."

She murmured in agreement. "A shame we couldn't have handled that before we left."

"Yeah. It just didn't work out that way."

"When is our rendezvous with our new ride?" she asked.

"Two days. I had the PAC base on Bennaris send a security team and the best ship they had available."

"Oooh. I like the sound of that. What is it?" She sat up straight, waiting eagerly for his reply.

"Class-six cruiser," he said.

"Oh." She felt slightly deflated. A class-six was a powerful, maneuverable vessel, but it lacked some amenities and was nothing special to pilot.

"Don't look so disappointed," he said. "You didn't let me finish. It's a Kiramoto class-six."

She stared at him. "Shut up."

He stared back at her mutely.

She realized what she'd said. "It's just a phrase. I didn't mean it. Say more words."

"What more is there to say?"

"Have you been on a Kiramoto six?" Kiramoto cruisers were luxury liners, usually either for private ownership or private charter, and always used only by the rich and the elite.

She'd sure never seen one in person, much less gotten to pilot one. Her skin tingled with anticipation.

"I could tell you," he began.

She held up a hand. "Enough. Fine. I will just be in awe of it all by myself because you're too cool to say anything."

He put his hand on her arm and gave her a jiggle. "Don't pout."

"I never pout."

"Fine. I haven't been on one either. Happy?"

She smiled. "Incandescently."

"Good. You can take the first shift on the bridge. I'm confident that those four are secure, but from here on out I want one of us on the bridge at all times. I'll relieve you in four hours."

She used his shoulder as a prop to push herself up to her feet. "Make it six. You look tired."

He smirked, but whatever response he had, he thought it instead of speaking it. He reached for the box that held the brivinium sphere.

"Wait!" she shouted.

He jerked back, startled. "What?"

"Thought I saw a spider," she said. "Never mind."

She laughed all the way to the bridge.

11

FALLON FELT a disproportionate sense of relief when handing off the smugglers and their ship for someone else to deal with.

Boarding the Kiramoto class-six cruiser, on the other hand, reminded her of going to the pastry shop when she was a kid and wanting to order one of everything.

It even smelled good. Like the faintest hint of cinnamon and something...expensive.

She had a hard time locking such a magnificent thing down to mere words.

"Look how happy you are." Minho smiled. "Want me to take your bag?"

"What? Why?"

"You're going straight to the bridge, right? I need to visit the necessary, and I'll drop our bags off in our quarters."

She paused then ducked her head under the strap of her bag and handed it to him. There wasn't much in it. It wasn't as if they'd had a chance to pack. Fortunately, the ship had been fortified with supplies they might need.

Was he giving her a chance to see the bridge alone? She

searched his face, but saw nothing to convince her one way or the other.

"I'll see you up there," she said.

He nodded and turned toward the ship's quarters and she continued alone to the nose of the ship.

Ah, the bridge of a Kiramoto was a thing of beauty. It was all sleek surfaces, elegant lines, and the best of materials.

Kiramotos weren't built with a budget in mind.

She indulged herself by taking slow steps around the entire space, sliding her hand over consoles and bulkheads.

Even the bulkheads had an understated sophistication to them.

Letting out a long sigh, she lowered herself into the pilot's seat at the helm and indulged in a long, satisfying stretch.

"Now this is a ship."

With great pleasure, she plotted and laid in a course to their next rendezvous—a handoff of the brivinium to the Briveen.

She'd received few details of what had happened on Asimov, except that the situation was under control. She didn't know if the lack of transparency was a matter of PAC intelligence not giving out information that wasn't strictly needed, or something more personal pertaining to her specifically. Wanting to keep her focused on her own duties, perhaps. At least they'd told her that Katheryn and Priestley had escaped it all unscathed.

So, whatever. If her job was now to fly this gorgeous ship, she wasn't about to complain that others had to deal with the trash fire Lydecker had started.

What an idiot. He'd had everything he'd needed to have a good, productive life, and he'd thrown it all away.

"Are we there yet?" Minho arrived, looking fresh. He'd changed into a simple black shirt and pants that must have been left in his quarters. She suspected he'd also taken a quick shower.

The amenities on the smuggling ship had been lacking, to say the least.

Actually, she could use a shower and change, too.

"Yes. ETA four days, two hours, and twenty-eight minutes." She stood and gestured at the seat. "Try it out. It's a pretty sweet ride. I think I'll go freshen up."

"Good idea." He crinkled his nose slightly, as if to suggest she had an aroma to her.

She snorted and accidentally-on-purpose bumped him with her shoulder as she passed by.

"I can't decide what I like more about this ship," Fallon said later, "the smoothness of the control functions or the autopilot."

She sighed in contentment. The past three days had been a delight. Outside of playing with the Kiramoto, she worked out, slept, played *Go* with Minho, and looked forward to reuniting with Hawk, Peregrine, and Raptor.

That reunion was going to be epic, and it was getting so close she could practically feel it under her skin.

"Why does everything have to be one thing or another with you?" Minho asked with good humor. "Why can't you just let things be what they are, without naming and sorting them?"

"That would be disorganized." She looked up from the helm to grin at him. "I like tidiness."

He smirked at her. "You're in the wrong line of work, then."

"Am I? Or am I about to bring a level of awesomeness to Blackout that has never been seen before?" She opened her eyes wide and stared at him.

They both laughed.

"One of these days," he announced grandly, "you're going to be a very big problem for PAC command."

"In a good way or a bad one?"

He straightened from his relaxed position in the copilot's seat. He shifted so he sat sideways, his knees pointed at her side. He leaned forward and waited until she turned to look at him. "Undecided. But for some reason, when I look at you, you always remind me of the ancient quote, 'Fools rush in where angels fear to tread.'"

As much as she hated to admit it, she didn't know that one. His joking tone had subsided and he now seemed deadly serious.

She shifted to meet him look for look. "I never aimed at being an angel."

He stared at her, unmoving, and it was only then that she realized how close they were. "Remember that," he said softly. "When the worst happens, remember that."

It was a strange moment. She felt like time was spiraling out away from the ship in every direction, but they were frozen together in the center of everything.

"Minho." She intended to follow that up with more words, but none occurred to her. She was too full of sudden questions.

"Not my real name," he said softly. "Even though it feels like it is."

What was he trying to tell her? He was always teaching her, preparing her for the future, but he'd never been so cryptic before.

"I don't understand," she said.

"Then don't try." He straightened and looked toward the exit, breaking the weird energy between them. "When you're ready, you'll understand without having to try."

She didn't like the feeling of this conversation. It felt like a warning.

"I'm going to get some sleep," he said. "I'll relieve you in four hours."

With that, he left, leaving her uneasy and uncertain.

FALLON SAT through her shift at navigation with an unsettled feeling. In less than two days, they'd meet the Briveen, hand off the brivinium, then await their new orders.

She expected to be recalled to Jamestown to rejoin Avian Unit. She hoped that Minho would receive the same orders.

She suddenly felt less confident about that being a possibility.

When he came to take a shift on the bridge, he'd returned to his amiable self, but she remained bemused. She went to the ship's small but plush gym and ran hard on a treadmill to tire her body and reboot her thought process.

She ran hard for a full hour, showered, and fell into bed.

Alarms woke her.

Leaping out of bed, she ran for the bridge before she'd even registered the time or the type of alarm.

Shaking off the haze of sleep, she burst onto the bridge, where Minho sat at the helm, leaning forward, shoulders rounded.

"What is it?" she snapped, throwing herself into the copilot's seat.

"Pirates. Intercept course. No response."

She looked at the voicecom to size up the situation for herself.

Blinking hard, she tried to clear her vision. What she saw made no sense.

"There are three ships." She stated the obvious because it was so improbable. Pirates didn't work together. They preyed on ships in major traffic paths.

She and Minho most definitely were not in any variety of traffic path. They'd arranged a rendezvous as far from anything as they could manage.

And yet, here were three ships, coming at them from different directions. She recognized the make of each immediately, and though they were all inferior to the Kiramoto, they had the advantage of numbers.

A Kiramoto class-six was immensely valuable. The pirates

probably had a setup that allowed a scout to relay information about potential targets.

However they'd been spotted, it was bad freaking luck.

Two ships of equal or lesser capability, she could handle.

"I can't outmaneuver these three ships with no backup." She said it flatly, feeling a disconnect with their reality. "They'll converge on us no matter what we do. They've positioned themselves so that wherever I navigate to, one of them will be able to intercept us. Even if we destroy them—and we probably have better firepower—they'll be able to delay us enough to allow the other ships to overtake us. How far out is the Briveen ship?"

"Too far." Minho's voice was grim. "We're on our own."

"Switch with me," she said, already moving toward the pilot's seat.

Minho rose halfway and slid around her, moving into the copilot's seat.

She called on everything she'd ever learned in every aspect of her life to aid her now. She calculated scenario after scenario, looking for any possibility of success.

She found none. Not even a weak hope of escape.

Taking a deep breath, she calculated another scenario. If she couldn't win, she'd work toward a different objective—a stalemate, to buy time.

"What are you doing?" Minho asked when he saw her consulting star charts of nearby systems.

"We can't win, but we can delay. Even with three ships, we can use their maximum speeds and maneuverability to plot a path for ourselves that will coincide with stellar phenomena. They'll have to alter course slightly, and we can delay their overtaking us."

When he looked over at her, his eyes dark and grim, she added, "All we have going for us is our superior ship and the fact that we have three axes to work with. If our only goal is to delay and evade, we can avoid a confrontation for approximately..."

She trailed off, pouring herself into her calculations.

"Thirty-eight hours," she finally said. "If the Briveen increase their speed beyond tolerance, they could make it."

She and Minho silently looked at each other. No words were needed.

Would the Briveen be willing to burn out their systems to reach them before the pirates could? It would mean putting themselves at extreme risk, since the Briveen would be brought into the fray with the pirates while on board a damaged ship.

"They're a deeply honorable people," he said softly. "Maybe."

Maybe. Their survival depended on an extreme that dangled on the end of an uncertain decision.

"You send the request to the Briveen. I'll set the evasion course." She focused on the task ahead of her, not indulging in any errant thoughts.

She heard him speaking, but tuned it out. If she sealed off all parts of the ship outside of the bridge, she could conserve energy that she could shunt into propulsion. Sure, the mechanical methodology was far from PAC-approved, but she wasn't too concerned about protocol at the moment.

She would have given just about anything for a good mechanic just then.

Over the next hours, she worked countless scenarios, adjusting energy output versus resource consumption while keeping them out of reach of the pirates.

"Forty-two hours," she finally said in a low voice. "That's the best we can hope for."

Had she come this far, only to go out like this? Minho's quiet gaze was somehow louder than the facts, saying that, perhaps, this was it.

She tried to imagine Peregrine, Hawk, and Raptor reuniting on Jamestown without her. Getting news of her demise. Trying to continue as a team without her.

No. It couldn't happen that way. She was their leader. She owed it to them to take care of them.

There had to be an answer somewhere. She didn't need much—just a few hours. All the information she had indicated that they'd exhausted their possibilities.

They had to find new possibilities.

As the hours ticked down, Minho grew quieter and more subdued. Neither of them slept. They kept digging, kept searching, for new answers, to no avail.

At thirty hours, he asked, "Have you created a message for delivery to your next of kin?"

A feeling of coldness pooled in her chest. "No."

"Go do it," he said. "Nothing's going to change here."

She hesitated.

"Go." He sounded colder and more authoritative than he ever had. "That's an order."

She went.

At twenty hours, Minho suggested she sleep, but how could she sleep away her remaining time?

"I wouldn't be able to fall asleep." She remained at the helm.

"So you're telling me that if we get a chance to make a stand, you're going to make me stand with someone who's sleep-deprived?" he asked.

She missed the old Minho, who joked even in dire situations.

"Tell me how," she said.

"If you can't put your team, me, and the PAC above your feelings, then focus your feelings on what you can do to serve them." His eyes were dark. Fathomless.

She bowed her head, then left the bridge.

In her quarters, she put on pajamas, as if she were going to bed on any other night. She brushed her teeth. She lay down and pulled the blanket up to her chin and imagined her mind as a one-way path from this moment to the next moment that she could help the PAC.

All she had to do was sleep. She closed her eyes.

AT TEN HOURS, Fallon ate. The food tasted like nothing, but it would flow through her blood and keep her strong.

At five hours, she ran more scenarios, but nothing had changed.

At three hours until the pirates closed in on them, she accepted that she and Minho weren't going to make it out of this.

She'd always expected to die as a Blackout agent. She just hadn't expected it to happen so soon.

"Who are you really?" she asked Minho. "There's nothing to protect now, is there? My birth name was Kiyoko."

She wanted him to see her—really see her.

He turned in his seat toward her, and she did the same. Their knees almost touched.

"Is that who you really are, though?" he asked. "Are you Kiyoko—whoever that was?"

She pictured her parents, her childhood home, and the fighting competitions she did growing up.

That girl was buried inside her like an insect preserved in amber, but Kiyoko was just an ingredient in what Fallon had developed into.

Nor would the people who knew her then recognize her. Other than bearing the same physical features, she didn't think she resembled the same quiet, removed girl who had only felt anything resembling passion when she was fighting or flying.

She hadn't had any close friends then. She'd recognized

herself as too different, and hadn't wanted to force herself into the mold of pretending to be like them.

"No," she said quietly. "I'm not Kiyoko anymore."

"Then who are you really?" He asked her the same question she'd asked of him.

"I'm Fallon."

He leaned forward and took her hands in his. "You are. And you're fantastic. And that's enough. Talking about where we once came from won't help us know each other any better than we already do."

She looked at their hands. "You're right."

He smiled. "Of course I am. That's my thing."

His gentle humor made her smile.

"I guess this is the time to tell you that I haven't hated knowing you," she said.

His smile bloomed into a grin. "I haven't hated knowing you, either. Much."

She laughed. Fallon and Minho wouldn't get maudlin and say a bunch of emotional crap. They would look at their target, take aim, and give it everything they had, until the end.

He looked into her eyes, still smiling, gave her hands a small squeeze, then let go.

"Let's get ready," he said. "We'll make it good."

"THE GOOD NEWS," Minho said, "is that the Briveen ship has been able to increase their speed enough to get here within an hour of the pirates pinning us down."

"The bad news," Fallon said, frowning at the voicecom showing the three ships, which continued to tighten their perimeter around the Kiramoto, "is that an hour is more than long enough for them to disable and board the ship, then kill us."

There was no doubt that killing her and Minho would be

their top priority, along with dealing minimal damage to the Kiramoto.

Minho nodded. "Our options are either to pretend to negotiate with them to buy time, or wait as long as possible and put up a fight. I know which one I'm voting for."

She smiled. "Make it two votes. We fight. There's no point in attempting negotiations. They can see that Briveen ship coming just as well as we can, and will assume it's coming to assist us. Besides…I'd always rather fight."

"At least we can bank on the fact that they'll be trying to disable us rather than cause significant damage to the ship." Minho slowly rubbed his hands together, deep in thought.

He murmured, "It's a shame we don't have a shuttle, or at least an evacuation pod or something. Anything to create a little confusion."

Fallon frowned in thought. "What about drones?"

His attention snapped to her. "What do you mean?"

"There are ten of them on board. Let me think for a second." She pursed her lips, thinking about how they could use the drones to buy them some time. While she was no mechanic, drones were fairly simple machines.

Working through the thought as she spoke, she said, "If I were to cross-connect them, I could control them all at one time. I could also boost the signal gain enough to emit an energy reading that could serve as a distraction to the pirates."

Minho straightened, his eyes making tiny, quick movements from side to side even though his gaze was unfocused. "We could make it look like a ship, suddenly coming out of nowhere."

"Nothing that big," Fallon said. "Even spoofing a shuttle's signal would require us to mount something to it that could generate a much bigger energy output. It wouldn't have to be tiny, because it would be out in space, but for maneuverability, it would need to be small. We don't have anything like that."

"How small?" he pressed.

"I'm not an engineer," she said. "I don't know how far we could push it. To be safe, I'd say about the size of your head, and weighing maybe two kilograms."

He stood. "I'll be right back."

She remained on the bridge, wondering what he was doing. His nervous energy suggested that he had an idea.

She really hoped he did.

He rushed back in and thrust something toward her. "How's this?"

She examined it, but she'd never seen anything like it. "The measurements seem good, but what is it?"

Shaped something like an eyeball, the item was encased in a smooth, black material.

"It's an EMP pulse bomb."

She stared at him.

He shrugged. "I asked for one to be put on the ship. Just in case."

"I don't really feel good about the fact that it's been here all this time and I didn't know," she said.

"Yeah, that's why I didn't mention it," he said maddeningly. "But it's far less dangerous than the brivinium," he pointed out. "This will only blow out electrical systems in the vicinity."

"Which would result in the deaths of everyone on these ships, including us," she noted, then paused. "Hang on. If we were already in containment suits when we set it off, we'd be able to survive until the Briveen got here."

She looked at him. This was a way for them to survive, but they'd have to kill everyone on those three ships.

He nodded. "That's exactly what I was thinking when you brought up the drone idea. Using the drone might allow us to get the thing far enough away that we won't experience a total power failure. If we make sure all three ships are within range, we can wipe them out and then wait for rescue. The Briveen could even tow the Kiramoto back for repairs."

She'd always known that being a Blackout operative meant she would eventually have to kill. Her thoughts went to the people on those ships. If they were all pirates, all willingly engaged in piracy in the PAC, then the deaths would be justified. But what if there were unwilling participants on board? Hostages, maybe. Passengers. Children, even.

They had no other choice but to take that risk, unless they wanted to die. She only hoped there were no innocents on those ships.

"How long will it take you to get the drones ready?" he asked.

"Ten drones, a minute each to link, then a few minutes to mount this." She cupped the EMP pulse bomb carefully in her hands.

"Okay. Go. I'll grab containment suits and we can help each other get them on when you're done. Meanwhile, I'll plan this out."

During her training to be a clandestine operative, she had often imagined a dire scenario like this. She'd wondered how it would truly feel, and how she would react. Whether the pressure might make her falter.

Without hesitation, she ran, clutching the pulse bomb to her chest.

A strange sense of power filled her. It shouldn't—she was far from being in a dominating position. In fact, she and Minho had been backed into a corner and forced to take extreme actions.

But the feeling that rose within her, first like a breeze then growing into a whirlwind, felt like power. Electricity.

It was way better than any physical battle she'd ever engaged in, or any flight she'd ever taken.

She felt more fully alive than she ever had, like all her latent senses had, at long last, roared into life.

She felt incredible. Limitless.

In the docking bay, she gathered the drones together on the floor and connected them, both physically and mechanically. The pulse bomb, she anchored in the center of them so that the entire structure was ball-shaped. She hoped to protect the most critical part as much as possible, in the event of space junk or some action on the pirates' part.

She finished the physical work, then put on her VR gear and carefully raised the multi-drone unit into the air, testing it to make sure it was fully operational.

It was.

She gently landed it on the floor of the bay. The maneuver was made particularly tricky due to its shape and the fact that the drones weren't intended to be used in that way.

Minho rushed in and dropped the containment suits. "Status?"

"As planned. It's ready."

"Good. Let's suit you up first."

While containment suits were designed so that a person could get into one on their own, it was a whole lot easier and quicker to have help.

Minho helped pull the suit up over her legs, pull it down over her arms, check all the internal mechanisms, then close it up. "We'll put the helmets on last."

She then helped him into his suit. Her hands didn't shake, and she didn't feel panicked. She felt really pleased with herself handling all this just as she'd always hoped she'd handle a major crisis.

"So what's the plan?" she asked.

"First," he said, "we'll eject the unit out into space. Then, you'll maneuver it out and take it as far as you can, as fast as you can, while remaining within range of all three of the ships. Ideally, we'll be able to wipe out all of their systems without completely burning ours out."

Inside the ship, the device would have been difficult to maneuver. Out in space, though, it wouldn't have gravity or walls to contend with, and the combined power of ten motors would give it some decent speed, for a drone.

Maybe this could actually work.

"And if anyone decides to open fire on it," she said, "we'll just activate it."

"Right. Are you ready?"

She nodded.

"Eject it, but don't activate it. I want us both sealed in on the bridge before that. I'll go up and prepare for power loss. I'll monitor the ships and adjust the drone's course while you pilot it."

After they helped each other with their helmets and double-checked their suits to make sure they were secure, Minho went to the bridge.

She loaded the drone device into the airlock then ejected it into space. It silently drifted away from the ship without fanfare.

As soon as she got to the bridge, she carefully put her VR gear on over her helmet. She had to fiddle with the straps to make that work, but eventually found a decent fit. Then she waited for Minho's signal.

"Now," he said.

She activated the drone and her vision became that of deep space.

She took a sudden, unexpected breath.

"Something wrong?" Minho asked.

"No. This is just…it's like I'm just floating through space." She knew, logically, that the view was only projected on the visor in front of her eyes, but VR images were so all-encompassing that they tended to fool the brain into believing what it saw.

She heard him behind her, calling out coordinates to follow, and she dutifully proceeded on that course. She couldn't see the pirate ships, but she felt their presence as they bore down on her.

"How long will it take for the drone to get far enough away from us?" she asked.

"At this speed, it would take an hour to get clear."

"And how far are the ships from pinning us in?"

He said airily, "Oh, about an hour."

"Great."

"That's why I'm going to alter course to move us back from it, as fast as possible."

"That will mean the other ships will intercept us faster," she said.

"Yup. But they'll make a beeline for us, drawing them in closer to one another, while also maximizing our distance from the EMP. Besides, who wants a long, drawn-out conclusion to such an exciting adventure?"

Since she couldn't see him and therefore couldn't give him a dirty look, she instead went the juvenile route and made a raspberry sound.

"Here we go," he said. A moment later, he added, "They've altered course. Adjust your x axis by plus two point three degrees."

She changed the heading. "Done."

After nearly a minute of silence, she asked, "How far?"

"In terms of time, about fifteen minutes."

"Any sign they've noticed the drone?"

"Not yet," he answered.

Minutes ticked by and just to put some conversation between them, she asked, "How about now?"

"Same."

So much for conversation.

Three minutes later, she asked, "When will we set off the EMP?"

"I'm watching the ships. So far, no energy readings suggest they've engaged their weapons systems. They're probably hoping to pen us in and get us to surrender in the hopes that they'll spare our lives."

"Who would fall for that?" she scoffed.

"You'd be surprised what people will fall for when the only other option is accepting that they're about to die."

"Okay," he finally said a moment later. "I think this is as far as we should push it. Are you going to watch this from in there or out here?"

She cut the drone's motors and pulled the VR goggles off her helmet. "There won't be anything to see. I'll watch it with you."

She stood next to him as he sat at the helm and triggered the EMP.

She held her breath.

Sensors showed the two ships closest to the drone blink out, going dark other than a fading glow of residual heat.

Then the lights in the Kiramoto went out. Fallon heard a loud crackling sound that lasted less than a second. The voicecom screen went dark before she could confirm the condition of the third pirate ship.

Minho's hands flew across the voicecom, but he shook his head. "Everything external is gone." A moment later, he added, "Everything internal, too. We got toasted, just like those other ships."

"Did you see the third ship go out?"

"No. But they weren't much further from it than we were. If we lost everything, then they probably did too."

Probably.

She didn't care for his use of that word. More specifically, she didn't care for the possibility of the improbable.

"So all we can do is wait," she said.

"Yep. Based on our last known position and that of the Briveen ships, they'll make it to us within the half-hour. At least we won't have long to wait."

"We should move to the docking bay," she said. "So we can get a look at whoever boards us."

He smiled faintly. "I was thinking the same thing."

They armed themselves with stingers and went to watch.

It was a peculiar feeling, not knowing if they were waiting for rescue or for slaughter.

A ship came into view. At first, it was too small to identify. Then it got larger and it was still too small to identify.

Then she saw that it was Briveen.

"If they're here and not fighting the pirates," she said, "that means we don't have to worry about the pirates."

"Stop stealing my thoughts," he said. "You're making this boring. We're supposed to be a wily duo, always bickering and disagreeing."

She squinted at him. "Have I ever told you that you're a strange man?"

She was glad for his odd sense of humor, though.

"Probably." He didn't seem to mind.

"I haven't met any Briveen in person before," she said. "Have you?"

The reptilian people tended to be xenophobic, and therefore rarely left the Briveen system.

"Yep. If you don't know the rituals, just bow low at the waist, like you would for an admiral, and stay that way. But keep your eyes up. Not maintaining eye contact is an insult."

She'd read that once. "I've read about the rituals, but I've never done them. I'll leave it all to you."

They watched the ship, many times larger than theirs, loom and dock.

When three Briveen came through the airlock, one by one, Fallon bowed, keeping her eyes up.

Then she noticed the stingers in their hands.

She jerked upright and reached to grab Minho's arm and haul him out of the cargo bay. Before she could take a step, her body froze, and she had a sensation of falling while everything went dark.

A HAND SHOOK her shoulder roughly.

Fallon groaned and tried to sit up, only to find a hand over her mouth. Everything that had happened flooded back to her and she fought to get free.

At least, she tried to. Her body felt like it was one open wound.

"Easy," a voice whispered in her ear.

Minho. It was Minho. She relaxed, and the cacophony of pain in her body subsided to a dull, roaring throb.

"I know you're hurt," he said. "Those stingers were set for Briveen, not humans. But we have four minutes right now, and we're not going to get this chance again."

His arms went around her waist and he gently put her into a standing position.

Her knees buckled.

"Okay. We'll do it this way." He crouched down and presented his back to her. "Just lean in and hold on the best you can."

She wanted to walk, but couldn't. She did as he told her. "What's wrong with me?"

He went to the door, already opened, and peeked out cautiously. "Your motor neurons are seriously screwed up right now. It will pass. Now hush."

He ducked into the corridor and hurried down the left side. She really wanted to ask where they were going, but the pain coursing through her and his order kept her silent.

At the end of the corridor, he entered a lift.

"Two decks down," he said.

"For what?" She rested her chin on his shoulder.

"Escape pods."

"What's going on?" she asked.

"I'm not exactly sure, but these aren't the Briveen we thought they were."

"Are they involved in the smuggling?"

"They're involved in something," he said. "As soon as they're sure they know everything we know, they'll make us disappear. So if we want to remain un-disappeared, we need to get on an escape pod and signal for help."

"Why aren't we being guarded?"

"Easy. It didn't occur to them that a human would be capable of regaining consciousness for at least five minutes, much less being able to walk. I heard one say it would take a couple of days for that."

She shook her head slightly, trying to clear it. All of this was coming at her too fast, and it wasn't making sense. "But they'll just recapture us from the escape pod. It won't outrun this ship."

"I have a plan for that. Don't worry."

"I have to admit, I'm worrying, just a bit."

He chuckled and patted her right knee, which was probably digging into his ribs, but he didn't complain. "Just one more thing for you to tell a great story about—the time you escaped from being a prisoner on a Briveen warship."

"Sounds like a good story." She turned her head and laid it on his back, closing her eyes. The lift was spinning, but she was pretty sure that was just her.

She didn't like how she felt, or that she didn't fully comprehend what was happening. "How are you fine?"

"You very conveniently made yourself a human shield when you tried to grab me. I barely got touched."

She'd intended to get him out of the bay, but apparently she'd protected him instead. At least something good had some of it, even if it meant taking all the stinger fire on herself. "But what about getting away from—"

Her words were cut off when the lift opened and he took off running.

She bounced slightly with his every step, and it jarred her

pain-wracked body. She concentrated on clamping her mouth shut and not making any noise.

"Here." He hit a panel and a massive door slowly slid open, revealing a tiny escape pod. He crouched, sitting her up in a chair and strapping her in. "You've launched into orbit from a planet's surface, right?"

"Yeah. Why?" She concentrated on focusing on his face.

"Because this is going to feel a lot like that." Satisfied with the straps, he nodded and stepped back. "You're going to pull a lot of G's to launch this sucker out of here and get some distance from the ship. It's going to hurt, in the shape you're in. Hang in there. It will only last a few minutes, and then you'll be fine. It's just nerve pain, not actual injury. Okay?"

"Okay."

He stepped back. "Remember what I said about taking care of your team. I'm glad I got to work with you. You gave me a chance to right the wrong I made with my own team."

"What?" Did he think they weren't going to make it, despite what he'd just said?

"We're out of time. Here we go." He stepped backward, back into the corridor. He held his hand up in an *okay* sign and the doors closed with her inside and him outside.

"No! Wait! Minho!" she cried, reaching for her straps to release them.

The weight of the universe crashed down on her and she couldn't move.

He'd launched her. He'd launched her, and stayed behind.

She clenched her jaw against the electrical storm of pain in her body, and the horror of what he was about to do.

He hadn't made an *okay* gesture. He'd been holding the little marble of brivinium between his thumb and forefinger.

A few minutes could feel like forever. But finally, the pressure on her body eased and she went weightless. The pain immediately eased to a dull ache and she reached for the voicecom terminal built into her seat.

There. She saw the ship. It was fine. She'd misinterpreted what she'd seen. He probably just wanted her out of the way so he could fight for control of the ship without the Briveen using her against him.

The ship flew apart in a bright light that flared, then almost immediately went dark. A minute later, her pod shivered around her and there was a sound like gravel hitting a window. The voicecom went blank, and all she could do was sit and listen to the debris.

Fallon learned to hate the words, "Good work," and, "Well done."

A series of debriefings had let her spool out everything she had experienced over the past ten months. Fallon learned about Lydecker's smuggling operation and how deeply it had gone. He had apparently intended to support a Briveen radicalist splinter cell, in order to amass unfathomable wealth along with an untouchable position on Briv.

Stupid. Those weren't things that were worth people's lives.

She listened to Admiral Krazinski with a sense of detachment. She had no official duties for the time being, and though her body had been healed on the ship that had answered the escape pod's beacon, she felt like her shoes were full of lead.

She took her meals in her room and remained there whenever her presence wasn't requested on official business.

The porthole in her quarters remained closed. She'd seen enough of space while drifting around in it for days, waiting for rescue.

Her belongings from Asimov Station had already been delivered. She'd put them, unopened, into a small closet.

Asimov had a new captain now. Some senior staff had been replaced, too. Katheryn and Priestley had received promotions.

Pacing around her quarters, she poured herself a cup of water, then ignored it. Usually, she engaged in hard exercise to clear her head and restore her focus, but she had no interest in it.

Nothing interested her.

She started to sit on the couch, but straightened when her door chime sounded.

What now? She was tired of people's well-intentioned offers to go eat or enjoy the boardwalk. They thought she was a transitionary security officer, waiting for her next position.

She didn't want to know them.

Taking a deep breath, she pulled her facial features up into a pleasant expression and opened the door.

When she saw her visitor, her mouth parted slightly in surprise. All of her artifice fell away and she suddenly felt raw and exposed.

"Going to let me in?" Hawk asked.

She stepped backward, giving him space to enter. He did, then doors closed behind him.

He looked the same. Same reddish-brown hair in the same short style. Maybe just a bit more tanned. Same build. Everything was the same, except for his blue-gray eyes. They'd always been hard, but the hardness seemed to have been sharpened to an edge.

"Bad, huh?" he asked.

Krazinski had ordered her not to share information about her mission with her team. No doubt he'd received the same orders.

"Yeah," she said. "You?"

He nodded slightly. "Pretty bad."

"Yeah," she echoed, softly.

There was nothing else that really needed to be said.

He raised an arm, curved at the elbow, and without hesitation, she moved in and put her arms around him. His arms closed around her.

FALLON'S QUARTERS on Jamestown were small, but by tacit agreement, Hawk stayed in them with her. They watched holo-vids, stayed up late at the pub, and slept in the only bed her quarters offered.

For the first time since arriving on Jamestown, she began sleeping through the night.

She tried teaching him to play chess, but he complained and accused her of cheating every time she executed a gambit, so they gave it up.

It made her laugh, though.

Three weeks after Hawk's arrival, they were arguing over whose turn it was to buy dinner when the door chime interrupted.

"Answer that," Fallon called, retreating to the necessary.

When she emerged, Hawk was standing at the door, blocking it, and not saying anything. Fallon nudged him aside so she could look.

Peregrine, looking just the same, with her hair in its customary long blond ponytail, looked at Fallon and smiled.

A big smile.

Fallon didn't even have to ask if things had been hard on her. That smile had said it all.

"What's good to eat here?" Per asked. "I'm starved."

"Why aren't you two wearing your bracelets?" Peregrine asked as they shoveled Bennite stew into their mouths and talked a lot without saying anything of consequence.

"I wasn't allowed to take anything personal," Fallon said. "I sent it here."

"And?" Peregrine prompted.

"Nothing. I'll go get it right now." Fallon wiped her mouth and prepared to stand.

Peregrine caught her arm. "We can go after we're done eating."

She fixed Hawk with a look. "So what's your excuse?"

"Uh," he said, "same as hers."

Peregrine shook her head as if disgusted, but Fallon saw the subtle signs of her partner's amusement.

Admiral Krazinski hadn't told Fallon when Raptor would arrive, but she'd assumed it would be within days, or maybe a week or two. She, Hawk, and Peregrine developed a routine of getting up, working out, having breakfast, then moving through the rest of the day.

Weeks passed, and Raptor remained absent.

Peregrine, like Hawk, remained in Fallon's quarters, though she slept on the couch. Even if she'd wanted to sleep in the bed with Fallon and Hawk, there simply wasn't enough room.

The three of them worked on absorbing their experiences, knowing they were all going through something, but never speaking of what.

Whenever Fallon thought of Minho, her chest felt like she was suddenly pulling lots of G's. Consequently, she endeavored to keep herself busy and keep herself occupied with her teammates.

"This is a nice station," Peregrine observed one morning at breakfast. "Everyone is very polite."

"Of course they are," Hawk said. "They never know when an admiral might be standing behind them. Personally, I'm bored. I'm ready for frat boy to arrive so we can get out of here."

Fallon smiled at the nickname Hawk had given Raptor at the academy. That felt like so long ago, even though it was only a couple of years in the past.

"I like Jamestown too," Fallon said. "There's always something going on."

"Oh, sure, team up against me." Hawk threw a napkin down in disgust. "That's it. I'm out of here." He gathered up his empty dishes and pretended to stalk off.

"Where do you think he's going?" Peregrine asked, watching him go.

"My guess is that he's just going back for more food, but doesn't want us to know that because we might tease him about how much he eats," Fallon said.

Peregrine nodded. "Sounds about right."

ONE OF THE things Fallon liked about Jamestown was that even though her quarters were small, she still had a hydro shower. She didn't need much more than that, really, now that she had three-quarters of her team back together.

As she washed off the sweat from her workout, she traced the tattoo on her abs, thinking about the matching versions imprinted on her partners.

Had Minho shared something like that with his team? Would he have agreed to get a tattoo if he'd been allowed to join Avian Unit?

She'd never know.

After repressing thoughts of him for weeks, he kept coming up in her mind, as if fighting back.

Minho wouldn't have allowed her to forget him. Nor would she, ever.

She hadn't even told Hawk and Peregrine about his death. It was the one thing she could say about her time away from them, and she hadn't been able to. Saying it out loud felt like it would truly be the end of him, as illogical as that was.

After drying off and pulling on a shirt and some soft, formless pants, she crossed the tiny bedroom where she could hear the others talking. "What do you think about ordering dinner in?" she asked. "I'm thinking—"

She froze. She could only see a person's back, but she knew that back. Every slope and angle of it. Even the freckle right at the small of his back, which was currently hidden by a PAC uniform.

Raptor turned, looked at her for a long moment, and his face creased into a smile. "Aren't you going to say hi?"

It seemed inadequate, but she nodded. "Hi."

"Is that it? I'm a little underwhelmed here. I've been imagining what it would be like for us to all get back together. In my head, it was all confetti and cheers, and, I'll admit it, a little bit of me being lifted up on your shoulders and carried around."

She laughed.

"These things never happen the way you imagine them," Hawk said.

"That's for sure," Peregrine added. "It's best just not to have any expectations."

"Oh." Raptor nodded slowly. "So…no cake?"

Hawk put an arm around Raptor's shoulders in a gesture that would have been fraternal, if his arm wasn't like a crowbar. "Damn if cake doesn't sound good. Let's go find one."

ALL FOUR OF THEM, now finally together again, slept in Fallon's living room that night. They spent the day together, then dispersed to their own rooms for the night.

In spite of the fact that they all had experienced some bad stuff, she finally felt whole enough to face whatever mission came at them next. She was sure they felt the same way, though all of them, when they thought no one was looking, sometimes wore a morose or bitter expression before covering it up.

She didn't mind having her quarters back to herself for a little privacy. Especially since she knew that Hawk, Peregrine, and Raptor were all just steps away. She still needed to go through her things from Asimov and sort them. Some things could be disposed of, and others might go into her storage compartment.

Realizing she hadn't checked her messages that day, she sat down at the voicecom and saw that Admiral Krazinski had sent her two messages, both in text form.

Odd.

She opened the first one, which had a file attached to it.

Fallon,

I've waited a little while to give you this, because I thought you needed some time. I hope that was the right choice. Now that you have your team back, I think you're ready.

Losing Minho was a great loss to all of us. He was easy to like, and you two must have grown quite close over the last couple of years. You weren't just an assignment to him. He listed you as his next of kin. All of his belongings have been put into storage, and you can go through them whenever you wish. He also left this video. No one has viewed it. It's only meant for you.

He was one of the best officers I've had the pleasure of knowing. He suffered after the loss of his team, but you gave him a second chance to save his teammate. I'm certain that he had no regrets, even though we have many for having lost him. He was a good man.

John Krazinski

She let out a slow breath. Minho had waited a long time to say whatever he wanted to say. She wouldn't make him wait longer.

She selected the attachment.

Minho's sudden appearance on her screen made her take in a sharp breath. There he was, alive and smiling, looking beautiful and kind with the crinkles that appeared at the sides of his eyes.

How could this man no longer exist?

"Fallon," he said, still smiling. "If you're getting this message, it means that you've graduated from my expert tutelage. You worked hard and I hope you learned a lot, and that what you learned will keep you alive for a very long time. I wish I knew how I died. Not just so I could, you know, keep it from happening, but also so I could say something pithy about my last moments and wrap it all up with some really profound words."

He grinned suddenly and her heart ached. "But life is never that convenient. All the wrong things happen at all the wrong times. We miss our chances. What matters, in the end, is that we lived each day giving our best to the PAC and the people we care about. If I died doing that, then be happy for me because it's what I truly want. It's what we all sign up for, after all."

His eyes dropped for a moment. "That's it, I think. Fight hard, and if something good comes your way, take it, even if it's only for a little while. Take all the good things while you can. They're all we get to take with us when we go. Thanks to you, I know I'll be taking some great things with me."

He smiled again, then tilted his head to the side thoughtfully. "You know what? If I'm dead, I might as well say something I never would have said when I was alive. Ready? I love you. Everything about you, from the way you laugh to the way you fight. Even your dedication to your team, which is why I never would have told you how I feel. But I didn't need to say it. You make life good again without declarations and all that."

The corners of his eyes crinkled. "It's kind of nice to get to say that. Weird, but nice. Almost worth dying for." He laughed. "Almost. Anyway...take care, Fallon."

The video ended.

Silent tears ran down her cheeks as she archived the message. She didn't want to see it again, but she wanted to keep it safe.

Tears landed softly in her lap, making wet circles as she moved on to the admiral's second message.

Report to my office at the beginning of the day shift for Avian Unit's new orders. It's time for you to get back to work.

She gave herself ten minutes to finish her mourning. *"Life is never convenient,"* Minho had said. *"I love you. Fight hard."*

She would fight hard, and make sure his sacrifice made a difference.

After her ten minutes were up, she steeled herself and went to sort her things from Asimov Station and put them away, rather than letting them remain in her closet. She had to get on with life.

She wouldn't forget Minho. The tea box she'd bought when she was with him would be a source of strength, not one of grief. She would make tea and think of him, and smile.

Eventually.

Meanwhile, she had her team to take care of, just as he'd taken care of her. No doubt they needed it, after whatever they had been through on their own missions.

She tightened her grip on the tea box and gently set it in her kitchenette.

In the morning, she'd find out what Avian Unit would do next.

"Blood and bone."

MESSAGE FROM THE AUTHOR

Thank you for reading!

If you enjoyed this story and can spare a minute or two to leave a review on Amazon, I'd be grateful. It makes a big difference.

Believe it or not, we've made it to the end of the series. The final book will show Avian Unit finally becoming what they were always meant to be. Be sure to grab *Out for Blood* for an action-packed adventure.

Be sure to visit www.ZenDiPietro.com and sign up for Zen's newsletter so you'll never miss a new release or sale. Stay tuned for more adventures!

I hope to hear from you!

In gratitude,
　　Zen DiPietro

ABOUT THE AUTHOR

Zen DiPietro is a lifelong bookworm, dreamer, and writer. Perhaps most importantly, a Browncoat Trekkie Whovian. Also red-haired, left-handed, and a vegetarian geek. Absolutely terrible at conforming. A recovering gamer, but we won't talk about that. Particular loves include badass heroines, British accents, Kpop music, and the smell of Band-Aids.

www.ZenDiPietro.com.

Printed in Dunstable, United Kingdom